Land of Outcasts

Land of Outcasts

~ Songs of the Wanderers: Book One ~

Josh Gauthier

Illustrated by Darby Mumford

LAND OF OUTCASTS

Cover design by Jess Koch

Edited by Claire Guyton

Interior design by Josh Gauthier

Author photo by Trish Hodgkins

ISBN 978-1-7361417-0-0 (hardcover)
ISBN 978-1-7361417-1-7 (paperback)
ISBN 978-1-7361417-2-4 (ebook)

First Edition: 2021

For everyone looking for the place they belong.

Contents

Elsewhere...

THE SERVANTS in Duke Fabar's manor knew that an order to keep to their rooms signified the imminent arrival of a visitor they were better off remaining as unaware of as possible—assuming that they valued their freedom and their lives. Because these particular servants—the ones not imprisoned or vanished in the dead of night—did indeed value the ability to continue drawing breath, there was no one to mark the dark shadow of a man passing through the manor like the chill that shivers down your spine without warning.

The man in black followed servants' passages between the walls, working toward the receiving room at the manor's center. He walked on noiseless feet and wrapped himself in shadows that concealed the weapons strapped across his body. With a face as inscrutable as an open grave, he pushed aside a painting to step into the receiving

1

room. Coals glowed from the grate, shining dim orange light into the otherwise dark room.

The space would have been ornate with half of the adornment—and it would have been stylish if someone with sense and restraint had been allowed to oversee its design. As it was, the visual affront of the room stirred distaste or alarm in those who encountered it for the first time. It suited Duke Fabar perfectly. As the man in black crossed a thick carpet which should have been deemed illegal for its excess, the only sound was the soft clink of fine china from the high-backed chair near the fireplace.

The duke jolted when he looked up to discover his guest standing within reach of his elbow. "Who—!" His squeak of a voice quieted as he recognized the other man. "Oh, Nix, you're here." The pale of fear did not leave the duke's face, even as he schooled himself back into a semblance of composure.

The man called Nix made no comment on the duke's demeanor. When he spoke, his voice was low, like thunder in the distance. "You have need of me?"

Fabar set aside his mug and saucer, the better to conceal the slight tremble in his hand. "Yes, yes. I have a job for you. I believe you know a pair of mercenaries named Eli and Sasha?"

A faint grin curled the edges of Nix's mouth. "I do."

"Well, they recently assaulted a caravan of… goods I was transporting. They massacred my guards—left them strewn over the mountain pass. The shipment was lost, and that damned pair have run off with my money. I want you to bring them to me—dead would be acceptable."

Nix heard the exaggeration in the duke's story. The lie would have been clear even if Nix hadn't been familiar with his new targets. But—and here Nix reached for a desperate hope—perhaps Eli had finally overstepped. Perhaps Nix's long-awaited opportunity had arrived. He did not let the thrill of this possibility show on his face. There was another matter to be dealt with first. Nix did not like being lied to. "My usual rate?" he asked. "Plus an extra hundred since the targets are obviously dangerous if they've carried out such a massacre."

The duke's expression tightened, but he reigned in his annoyance at the haggling. "Plus a bonus for swift completion," he added instead. Clearly, this was a matter the duke wished brought to a rapid conclusion if he was being so free with his money. "I have already issued a general bounty," he continued, "but I have little faith in the usual sell-swords."

"Do you know where they are now?"

"My spies claim they are fleeing south."

"If they're on the run, I expect they're making for The Green."

Fabar grimaced. "Where all scum and miscreants end up. Will that be a problem?"

"Not at all. I will report back when it's done."

~ ~ ~

The duke never enjoyed these little encounters. People like Nix were like weapons—best kept at a distance and handled by other people. But this situation required a personal touch.

3

He blinked when he realized the mercenary was no longer standing beside him. The man tended to do that—appearing and vanishing without warning. Settling back into his chair, he listened carefully for the sound of the painting being shut. When no sound came, he leaned around to look. The portrait hung in its usual position, and there was no sign that Nix had ever existed.

Alone in the dark, Duke Fabar shivered. He retrieved his tea from the side table and willed it to stop shaking. Soon—

Soon, this would all be just an unpleasant memory.

Chapter 1.
A Much-Needed Vacation

ONE OF the most distinctive characteristics of the region known to most as The Green is its smell. Unfortunately, for those who have the misfortune to find themselves in this part of the world, the smell is, quite plainly, abhorrent. And if the odor pervading the bogs and wetlands at the southern edge of the continent is not enough, visitors quickly come to appreciate the other notable qualities of the region—carnivorous insects, fetid pools of water, oppressive humidity, and a wide array of aggressive natural species.

Three kinds of people exist in The Green.

The first kind are born there. Life in The Green provides little opportunity for accumulation of wealth or social advancement. Those born south of the fens, with very few exceptions, also die there—leaving their moldering houses and paltry livelihoods to their children.

The second group of people are those forced to The Green by circumstance—criminals, debtors, and those who find themselves with no other option. In due time, this second group adds to those in the first, and so the cycle continues.

The only other people in The Green are known locally as "the visitors." Bounty hunters, agents of business, opportunists—these come to The Green in search of money, and they tend to leave quickly.

Or they vanish, just another memory lost amidst the trees.

However, on a humid day so thick you could almost swim through the air, a man walked along the wooden causeway toward the small town of Harman's Folly, and he did not fall easily into any of these categories. Meanwhile, the great black horse walking beside him—which was not actually a horse at all—was a creature unlike any ever before seen in lands so far south. At eighteen hands, she stood taller than an average man. The horse-that-was-not-a-horse had shaggy black hair matted with burrs and mud. Sticks tangled in her mane and tail, and her saddlebags had grown loose, leaning awkwardly to one side.

But the horse's most notable feature—the thing anyone with eyes would notice first—was the black horn jutting from the center of her head—marking her, not as a horse at all, but as a unicorn.

"Tell me again why you dragged us down here?" asked the unicorn in a voice that was undeniably female, but also low and rough, carrying little warmth.

The man took a deep breath of putrid air and held back a gag. "Warm temperatures, beautiful scenery, abundant opportunity—what's not to like?"

The unicorn turned her head from the endless swamplands to the five-foot lizard hissing at them from a nearby branch. "You're right, Eli," she drawled, "this is obviously the most beautiful place I've ever seen. Thank you for bringing me here."

Eli inclined his head as though the thanks were sincere. "You're welcome."

The unicorn snorted, closing her eyes slowly before speaking again. "Back home, I had an ancient forest that whispered secrets in the dead of night. I had spreading grasslands where I could run for hours, wide battlefields where enemies cowered before me. And we've given it all up for this."

"We gave it all up because we made a powerful man quite angry. I won't speak for you, but I'm rather partial to breathing." Eli said with a smile. "Besides, I think it's beautiful."

The unicorn fixed one golden eye on him. "Your neck is bleeding from a nasty looking bite. You have sweat soaking through your jacket, and there are a pair of eyes watching us from the water, just down there. I expect the creature attached to them is more than ready to eat us both if the opportunity arises." She sniffed. "Well, you at least."

Eli sighed. "Sasha, really, can't you just enjoy the moment?" He spread his arms, turning in a circle to take in the view. "When will we ever see a place like this again?"

It was only a flash in the dim light, but something lunged at the tail of his coat as it flared beyond the edge of the walkway. Eli leapt away to the sound of a growl and a splash that sent muddy water spilling across the bridge.

Sasha laughed. "Well, maybe this trip will be good for a little entertainment if nothing else—so long as it's brief. We aren't staying, right?"

His breathing shaky in the immediate aftermath of nearly being eaten, Eli tugged his hat lower, his composure settling back into place almost immediately. He straightened his coat—and the two flintlock pistols secured beneath—and resumed walking down the causeway without answering.

"Wait, Eli. We aren't staying? Eli!" The unicorn followed at an anxious trot while her metal shoes left gouges in the rotting planks of the walkway.

~ ~ ~

Harman's Folly was a rickety little town perched atop a series of knolls in a patch of swamp that at one time and by at least one person—presumably named Harman—had been selected as less off-putting and hostile than the rest of The Green. Of course, the town was also named Harman's *Folly*, leading to the entirely possible alternate theory that Harman had selected the location for less sensible reasons—and to the closely related suspicion that Harman had been an idiot.

Whichever history is to be believed, the only goodwill the residents of Harman's Folly held for their home was the stubborn pride of those who have nowhere else to go and are ready to fiercely defend their own against any who dare intrude.

There were few in the settlement who missed the arrival of the strange man with the broad hat and the tall unicorn that followed him. In these parts, strangers were rare and often unwelcome. And unicorns—well, they inhabited children's tales and the rumors of distant lands, passed from mouth to mouth until the truth was little more than a kernel nestled amidst a drunk's slurred ramblings. Tales of unicorns were often followed by reports of dragon armies, dancing tree spirits, benevolent nobles—and other such ludicrous ideas.

Eli followed the main walkway to the knoll occupying the central point of the village. Where the bridge ended, a

worn path crossed the cropped, thick grasses that grew in abundance throughout The Green. The buildings that lined the path—locals called it a street—were multi-storied and leaning, built of crooked boards slowly rotting away in the sticky heat.

Eli spied a general store, an apothecary, a healer of some sort, and a three-leveled tower perched on stilts at the edge of the knoll. The tower seemed likely to serve as a seat of power for whoever held the mantel of leader in this quaint, little village. He assumed this mainly from the fact that someone had made an attempt at detailed wood carving on the railings and other fixtures of the wooden tower—though they had clearly given up before completion. Also, the way that the tower's ongoing expansion had begun to cannibalize the building next to it seemed a particularly apt representation of typical leadership.

The only lingering thought Eli gave to any of these buildings was a mental note not to do anything requiring a trip to the healer's. The row of headless snakes hanging from the porch roof was not quite up to his usual standards. He certainly wasn't about to admit it to Sasha—she'd never let him hear the end of it—but it was increasingly becoming clear how much one, little decision was going to cost them. And the full cost was still to be counted.

Yet Eli saw no way things could have gone differently. So often in his life, matters were simply out of his hands. He merely followed the road wherever it led. And right now, the road led down a narrow street lined with the inhabitants of Harman's Folly—every one of whom had noticed their arrival and stood watching.

The building Eli was most pleased to locate was the low-lying structure perched over the swamp with an attached dock and a hand-painted sign offering "Abasi's Food and Drink" with an arrow pointing down the slope to the doorway. Their rations were running low, and Eli had hardly eaten anything all day. He very much looked forward to sitting indoors and enjoying a meal that was neither smoked nor salted.

Unfortunately, the path to the tavern was blocked by a gang of five men who had taken up position in the center of the street. They were simply armed—with clubs and staves and knives—and wore no armor, though they looked formidable enough at a glance and were heavily muscled to a man.

Eli—though not weak by any measure—was slight of person and not particularly intimidating in appearance. He still disputed this, but Sasha had pointed it out enough that he had to admit there might be at least a little truth to the claim. When the leader of the motley band stepped forward, smacking his club into his off-hand—likely intended as intimidation—it became clear that the men were not about to let Eli and Sasha pass without inconvenience. Honestly, all Eli wanted was food, a drink, and five minutes' peace. Was that too much to ask? He pulled his coat tighter, concealing his weapons, and continued forward.

"You there, visitor," said the leader—a stocky man with sparse, sandy hair and a jagged hole of a mouth. "Is that a real unicorn?"

"Eli," Sasha asked in response, loud enough for the men to hear, "is that a pig in the street ahead? It's difficult to tell sometimes."

The leader growled, but Eli merely shrugged. "I didn't tie that horn on if that's what you're asking."

"We could get good money for a creature like that," said the man. It was at this point Eli decided he didn't much care for the stranger—a fact he confirmed when the man continued by adding "alive or sold off piece-by-piece."

Well, so much for resolving things peacefully. Eli slipped his hands into his pockets. "I wouldn't say things like that if I was you."

"Or what?"

"I just wouldn't do it."

"Well," said the man, "it don't matter much what you think. Now step aside and let us take that beast for ourselves."

Sasha watched the would-be bandits quietly. All around them, curious eyes observed from open windows and creaking storefronts. Eli didn't raise his voice or shift position. Aspiring outlaws like this were a little like chickens—you had to speak calmly and not make sudden moves in order to avoid spooking them. "Listen, friend, I'm not looking for a fight. I'm just trying to make sure you understand what you're asking. Have you really thought this through?"

"Little man," said the leader, "the unicorn's coming with us one way or another." One of the brutes at the back of the group held a heavy rope already looped to go around Sasha's neck. "The only question is whether we're gonna' have to spill your brains on the street before that happens."

Why did they never take the hint? "Are you sure you can handle her?"

"Shut up and get out of the way." The leader stepped forward, leveling his club at Eli's face across the distance separating them.

Eli was trying to do them an undeserved favor. He held out his empty hands but didn't back down. "We're not looking for trouble. Let's just part ways here and forget this ever happened."

The man moved closer. "One more word and you'll have more trouble than you care for."

Eli looked at Sasha—at the muscles taut beneath rough black hair and tough skin, at the raised scars that crisscrossed her flesh, at the sharpened metal shoes nailed to her feet. A jagged scar ran down the side of Sasha's face, right across her milky white eye. She stood taller than Eli by a fair measure and every inch of her was iron-tested battle unicorn.

Eli looked back to the sandy-haired man whom he was now certain had a death wish. He couldn't possibly be this stupid otherwise. Eli did quick calculations—two knives, three clubs, two staves, one rope—and not a trained stance among them. He didn't want to fight, especially if he didn't have to—and this was one fight Eli didn't have to participate in. "Fine," he told the group. "She's all yours."

The leader blinked his surprise, but Eli ignored him.

"Really, Eli?" He heard Sasha's mutter, but didn't stop as he circled around the men—keeping one careful eye on their movements—and made his way down the hill into the dingy tavern.

The girl behind the bar couldn't have been more than twelve—though The Green had already taken its toll on her skin, her teeth, her hair. She smiled at him as he entered, and though there was a nervousness to it, Eli decided the expression fit her well. At least someone here gave a pleasant-enough welcome.

"What can I get you?" she asked as he slid onto a stool at the bar. When it didn't break beneath him, he asked, "What do you serve?"

The girl shrugged. "Most everyone 'round here just drinks snapper piss." She blushed faintly at Eli's hesitation. "Excuse me, that's what we call it at least. There was a man came through once said it was almost like the ale you probably have back home—wherever it is you come from."

"Well," Eli told her, "I guess I'll give it a try. And some bread and butter if you have it."

"I can give you bread, but you'll not find butter here."

"That'll do just fine."

The girl nodded and turned away to fill a dented mug from a keg on the counter. The tavern was spacious, but nearly empty at this time of day. Two old men sprawled across a table in the back corner—mugs, plates, and a ruined deck of playing cards scattered around them. One snored in little whistles that reminded Eli of a guard captain he had once embarrassed up north.

At the opposite end of the bar, a woman sat reading a ratty little book as she twirled a strand of dark-red hair around one finger. Eli's gaze paused on her, mainly to look for weapons, though he did allow himself a moment to appreciate the curves of her slight figure. Hers was not the refined beauty of high-born ladies in the north. It was natural and true—more striking in its honesty. The woman did not look up, and Eli did not allow his gaze to linger long. They had not reached the end of their road just yet.

Even as he examined the room—who knew a bar stool could feel so wonderful?—he mostly listened for sounds from the street outside. As the girl set the mug in front of him, he heard the first of the shouts. One of the drunks in the back mumbled something and rubbed his nose without waking. When the girl set Eli's food next to the mug, he heard Sasha whinny. This was followed by the first *thud* of a body hitting the ground. The bread was dark and crusty, but still warm; it was almost good.

It would have been a welcome change, Eli thought as he ate, to simply arrive in town and order a meal without all this unnecessary difficulty. Why couldn't they have accepted his favor and saved everyone a lot of trouble?

The screams started a moment later. Orders turned into pleas for mercy. Begging was silenced by a crash of breaking wood. It seemed a fair estimate that they hadn't kept up an orderly attack for more than a minute. Shame, really, that it always came to this.

With a final crash, silence fell outside. Eli sipped his drink. It was strong and thick, with an odd aftertaste that clung to the roof of his mouth—but not as horrid as he had prepared himself for. The girl behind the bar stared at the doorway in the sudden quiet, and even the woman at the end had stopped turning the pages of her book. Eli waited, counting seconds until he heard the familiar *thud-thud thud-thud* of Sasha's metal horseshoes descending the steps into the tavern. Judging by her gait, she had enjoyed herself.

The serving girl now gawked openly, her mouth hanging open and her eyes wide. The woman flicked an eye up to peek over the edge of her book. "Mister," the girl said, "your... horse can't be in here."

"Do I look like a horse to you?" Sasha bumped a stool aside to stand near Eli. "Well?"

"No," the girl finally squeaked out.

"Very good." The unicorn let out a snort. "Horse, indeed."

"Sasha, be nice," Eli murmured. "What's your name, girl?"

"Jaylin."

"And where are your parents? I'm guessing you don't manage this whole place yourself."

"My dad is Abasi, like it says on the sign. They let me watch things during the day when it's quiet, but they're about." Jaylin offered a vague gesture at nowhere in particular.

"Good girl. Now, Jaylin, I need you to get the biggest bowl you have and fill it with snapper piss"—Sasha gave him a sideways look at this—"and give it to my friend here. Alright?"

The girl nodded and disappeared through a door behind the bar.

16

"Snapper piss?"

"It's not bad." Eli took another drink. "You just have to get used to the consistency and the flavor."

"Delightful."

Sasha was clearly unharmed, but Eli was mildly concerned about the men still outside. "Are they still alive?"

Sasha let out a sigh. "Yes, sir. As requested, all five cretins are still breathing—though a couple may not walk straight again. Thank you for your assistance, by the way. I deeply appreciate it."

Turning away, Eli tapped his cup and said nothing. Sasha knew how he felt about such things.

"Really?" she asked. "You have to admit they had it coming this time. If you really didn't want me to fight, you could have pulled out the Furies and scared them off."

It was true—this fight was not Sasha's fault. He couldn't blame her—and she shouldn't blame him. To ease the tension, he flashed her a smirk. "And deprive you of your fun?"

"It was fun." If Sasha had been a human rather than a unicorn, she would have been grinning, her lips twisting and drawing back to reveal her teeth. It was an expression that had struck Eli as unusual when he first met her. Now, he hardly thought twice about it. The faces she made at him were the least of his concerns.

Jaylin returned with a bowl and filled it from the keg as well. As she set it on the bar, Eli drew two silver pieces from his coinpurse and slid them over the counter. With a flick of the girl's wrist, the coins vanished.

Sasha sniffed at the bowl. "What is this?"

"I didn't ask." Eli ate a second piece of bread. It was baked from some sort of grain he had never encountered before, its flavor somehow bitter and sweet all at once. After the initial adjustment to its quality, Eli found he might actually be enjoying it—though perhaps he was just hungry. Meanwhile, Sasha was still studying her bowl.

"Just drink it."

She sniffed again and took a taste before snorting and fixing a glare on Eli with her good eye.

"It's good, isn't it?"

"I really don't like you."

"Ah, come on. You'd be bored without me."

"I'd still be back home without you. Instead, we're in the middle of The Green, hiding from bounty hunters and drinking snapper piss."

"Sasha." Eli murmured the warning as he looked around the room again—first at Jaylin and then at the woman. Neither appeared to be listening—which was good. There were enough people involved in their business as it was.

Sasha said nothing—only dipped her mouth back into the bowl and began to slurp down whatever it actually was that Jaylin kept in the keg on the counter.

Chapter 2.
A Warm Welcome

THE SCENE outside the tavern wasn't terrible—as far as brutal beatings tended to go. Still, Eli wasn't entirely pleased with how their arrival had turned out. Beside him, Sasha flapped her lips as though trying to dislodge the lingering taste of her drink. "You know," he said, "that's a very horse-like expression."

Her mouth stopped moving. "I've killed men for lesser insults."

Eli grinned as he wiped sweat from his forehead. The air was nearly solid here. Every movement felt slow as the essence of The Green soaked through his clothes—through his flesh and into his bones. He'd probably start growing moss next.

He crossed his arms and turned back to the blood-stains drying into the dirt. Most of the weapons he had counted earlier now lay abandoned, though their owners had either fled or been dragged off—all except for the sandy-haired leader who was sprawled upside-down against the wall of a nearby shack, a massive bruise covering the side of his face and a trickle of spit dangling from the corner of his mouth. Eli tallied three broken signposts, a shattered barrel, and a—

"Sasha, is that a finger?"

Sasha sniffed. "Possibly."

That wouldn't win them any favors with the town's inhabitants. It was only a matter of time before someone came after him asking for money because of all this. They might even deserve it. He doubted that everything damaged belonged to the would-be thieves. "Do you recall that whole conversation we had about trying to make a good impression?"

She rounded on him, nostrils flaring. "You imply one more time that this mess was my fault, and I—"

Eli held up his hands. He already regretted pushing the issue. "You're right, you're right. Apologies. It's been a long journey. We're both tired, and I'm not giving you your due." It was hard to think in the heat and beginning their stay with a fight left his stomach unsettled and had him looking over his shoulder even more than normal.

Sasha held his gaze for a moment. "Apology accepted. Now, what are we—?"

As she asked her question, she didn't see the young man approaching on her blind side. "Friend," Eli interrupted, "you'll want to take two large steps back and ask permission to approach."

The youth, who was dressed passably better than most townsfolk Eli had yet seen, froze mid-step—looking from Eli to Sasha. The unicorn had gone tense, suddenly aware of the other's proximity. Honestly, it was Eli's fault for distracting her with his half-accusation. Her eye narrowed as she rounded on the newcomer.

"Begging your pardon, sir," said the lad, but Eli cut him off with a raised finger.

"It's not me you need to be begging the pardon of. It's her."

The young man looked at Sasha and seemed to shrink a little under her gaze. "Begging your pardon... ma'am," he offered. "But the town overseer requests that you join her for an audience. Both of you, that is. If you please."

Eli watched the messenger shrink a little more with each word.

"Do you hear that?" asked Sasha, her tone biting. "We've been invited for an audience."

"It's only just on the other side of the knoll," Eli told her. "Try not to sound so put-out."

Sasha snorted.

"We will meet with the overseer," Eli told the young man. "Lead the way."

There were even more people visible now that word of their arrival had spread. Eli supposed his presence was probably the most excitement they had had in some time. It could not be often that someone as accomplished as him passed through. He could hardly fault people for being curious.

And the presence of a unicorn might possibly be something of a novelty as well, if he was being totally honest.

A cluster of old women watched from beneath an overhanging roof, a gaggle of children peered around the corner of a larger house, and scowling men had taken up position in their doorways with weapons near at hand—though they seemed content to observe without making a nuisance of themselves. Sasha tended to have that effect on people.

The overseer did indeed occupy the leaning tower that Eli had noticed earlier. The young man who had fetched them continued up the stairs and into the building without pausing to address the hulking sentry just outside the door. Shirtless, the guard's dark skin glistened with some sort of oil that Eli supposed kept the insects at bay. He'd have to see about finding some of that oil for himself. As he followed their guide through the door, Eli slapped at something that was trying to burrow into his neck.

"No animals inside."

Eli closed his eyes and bit back his exasperation at the guard's words—then stepped back outside before Sasha offered her own response.

"Really?" the unicorn asked, looking to Eli. "Are we going to have to deal with this level of ignorance every building we enter? At least back home they had some respect."

"I'll take care of it." Eli turned to the guard who stared down at him. "Listen, she's not... an animal." Alright, maybe she technically was. He had never had to consider the question before. The guard didn't blink. "Regardless, she doesn't take kindly to being excluded."

"No animals."

Just once, Eli wanted to get through a day without needless conflict. It was all inconvenient, but letting Sasha bludgeon the overseer's bodyguard into unconsciousness would be even more problematic than usual. He crossed his arms and tried to stand a little taller. It didn't work. "Well, then, the overseer will just have to come out here to meet with us."

A woman's voice cut off whatever the guard's response would have been. "It's okay, Merrick. Let them both in."

Without a word, the guard's eyes went back to watching the street. It was probably too much to hope for an apology. Eli motioned for Sasha to follow him. "Careful of the floor."

The overseer was waiting for them in the foyer. She was a woman of roughly fifty years who carried a lifetime of authority in her stance. Her red hair going white was pulled back, and her clothes—skirt and sleeveless top— were simple but clearly of quality make. "Well," she said, looking over Eli and Sasha, "more northerners come to stick their noses into our business."

People in The Green were turning out to be even more welcoming than Eli could have hoped.

He glanced down to make sure that Sasha's shoes were not cutting into the floor and that they hadn't tracked anything too unseemly into the house. Sasha had set Eli on her blind side, so there was no worry about her getting annoyed at his "mothering." He was equally grateful for her silence this time.

"I first assumed you were bounty hunters," the woman continued, "but I'm reconsidering that assessment."

She had a no-nonsense attitude about her and a confidence that left Eli not wishing to test her unnecessarily— even with the dismissive tone in her voice.

"We're not here for bounties," Eli answered. He hesitated to say more. Coming here was the right choice—he had spent the past week convincing Sasha of that fact—but their current situation was still delicate. "We are taking our rest as we explore future possibilities."

"Out of work mercenaries then," the overseer said. "And probably in disfavor back home. It's no matter to me where you came from so long as you don't make trouble in my town. My name is Dalia, and my only concern is making sure that life here goes as smoothly as possible for the people under my protection, is that understood?"

"We—" Sasha started to say, but Eli cut her off.

"I imagine we wish to avoid problems as much as you. All we're looking for is a place to rest after our journey."

Dalia ran her eyes over the pair of them once more. "I don't imagine you'll have much luck laying low with an animal like that at your side," she said. Eli elbowed Sasha to silence her retort, so the unicorn just flared her nostrils in displeasure. "But if you keep the peace, we shouldn't have any problems with each other." With the brief interrogation over, the dismissal in Dalia's voice was clear.

"We thank you for your hospitality." *Such as it is.* Eli inclined his head to Dalia in parting.

The unease in his chest had grown from discomfort to full roiling—yes, that was the word. He didn't like the way she looked at them—the unspoken challenge behind her hard expression. Until proven otherwise, Eli assumed everyone he met was hiding dire secrets. It had helped keep him alive, but he could not deny a slight truth to the concern voiced by others that he had grown a mite paranoid with age—

—though the last person who told him that had tried to knife him the next day. Regardless, there was no doubt Duke Fabar had already placed a tidy sum on their heads. That alone was enough reason to keep their heads down while he figured out their next move. They were in The Green to avoid trouble, and Eli had every intention of pulling off that plan without interruption. The issues they had faced so far notwithstanding.

He felt Dalia's gaze burning into his back before the door snapped shut to separate them.

Chapter 3.
The Makings of a Plan... Almost

BY THE time they made their way back to the tavern, Jaylin's parents had returned from "about." After speaking with Abasi, Eli secured himself a room on the second floor of the tavern.

Though room was a generous term. It was little bigger than a storage space and did not lock.

Abasi himself was a small man of stocky build with a pleasant enough face, but Eli caught glimpses of fire behind the smile. Jaylin's mother, meanwhile, was taller and thinner, with a pinched, unhappy face at odds with her unshakably gracious demeanor. A bit of silver and the couple made sure Eli had everything he needed before leaving him to his own interests.

Eli and Sasha took their dinner in the common room—subjected to the poorly hidden stares of the rest of the tavern's patronage, as if they hadn't seen enough during the day. The way people continued to cluster in—while still leaving a notable space around Sasha and Eli—it seemed doubtful that they had come for the food.

The red-haired woman from earlier had relocated to a corner table, her booted feet up on a chair as she read and picked at a meal of what appeared to be part of a large snake. Eli pulled his attention away from wondering what her voice sounded like when he realized he was being watched by a rough-dressed man who was missing half his nose. As soon as the man noticed Eli's attention, he went back to his rowdy card game and did not look their way again for a while. Plenty of others continued to gape in his stead.

"If I get a disease from this place," Sasha grumbled, "I will forever hold you responsible."

The air around them was thick with woodsmoke that couldn't find the motivation to rise to the ceiling. The scent of roasting meat—normally a delight—could not completely cover the stagnant odor of the swamp just outside. As his coat continued to cling to his arms, Eli finally tossed the jacket off in hope of some relief. No one looked too long at the pistols hanging at his sides, but he knew their presence would not go unmarked. He just hoped Sasha's display at their arrival would keep anyone else from starting trouble.

"Relax," he told the unicorn. "It's not quite up to your usual standards, but these people get by well enough."

"Eli," said Sasha, fixing her eye on him. "Have you looked around? Half the people in this room are sick with something. No one is supposed to live in a place like this. No one. So now would be a wonderful time for you to share whatever halfwit plan you've come up with. I know you have one, and I'd just as soon get it over with."

Eli's initial plan already sounded pathetic in his head, and he knew it would sound even worse once crammed into words. And then Sasha would stomp on it, just for good measure. "The plan is to find some work."

The steps beyond that were still a work in progress.

Sasha blinked once, twice. "Find...work? What are you talking about?"

Now was the time to sell it—or very quickly come up with a way to preserve his own well-being against an angry battle unicorn. "You know as well as I that we can't go home anytime soon—can't go anywhere civilized really unless we are prepared to spend every moment looking over our shoulders. If we lie low here, chances are good that things will settle down up north. In the meantime, we can take a couple odd jobs to pass the time and keep our supplies up. A few months, maybe a year, and we'll be home free."

"Please tell me you didn't just say we have to stay here a whole year?"

"They're rough numbers," Eli told her. "It's hard to know at this point."

When Sasha opened her mouth to retort, he hurried to clarify. "I expect we'll be out of here long before then."

"And what's to stop the duke from sending someone to track us here?"

"He's welcome to try. The Green is massive, sparsely populated, and not welcoming to visitors. Anyone who follows us will have their work cut out for them."

"And when rumors of a unicorn and a stupid mercenary working The Green start circulating, what then?"

"Sasha," Eli drained his drink and coughed as it burned his throat. "Think back, how many stories did you ever hear come out of The Green in a timely manner?"

"Enough," she retorted.

"Few enough," Eli corrected. "The only people who bring back reputable stories tend not to be reputable people. How long did it take us to track down that—what was her name again? That woman who liked to burn down public toilets while her enemies were in them?"

"Weeks." Sasha groaned at the memory. Perhaps Eli wasn't helping his case by bringing up his past plans. He ran with it anyway.

"Exactly, weeks, and she stayed at the edge of The Green. We're very good at what we do. It'll be far longer for someone else—if they can manage at all. Unless you want to leave the continent or turn bandit in some dank, spider-infested cave, this is as good a bet as any."

"Easy for you to say. You're not the one sleeping in the stable."

"You've slept in stables before."

"This one smells funny." Sasha sniffed. "Everything smells funny here."

When the unicorn returned to her meal without flipping a table, Eli decided that his work was done—for the moment at least. Now, he just had to figure out the rest of his plan.

Chapter 4.
A Halfwit Plan

ONCE SASHA was grudgingly settled into the nearby stable—a small building shared only by two donkeys and a young stablehand whom Sasha cowed into submission with a string of creative insults and wide-ranging demands—Eli retreated to his room.

The narrow room contained a cot that creaked and a small table that leaned sideways on uneven legs. Someone had left him a bowl of water for washing. It looked clear enough at a glance despite smelling faintly sour. When he was finished though, an oily feeling clung to his skin that would not wipe away. Dropping the washrag in defeat, he repeated his internal mantra of late. This was the right choice. There was no better option. They were where they needed to be.

But repeating these things didn't make present circumstances easier, and it certainly didn't tell him what to do next. Sasha would not take kindly to an incomplete plan for long. Checking once more that his pistols were in easy reach on the table, Eli blew out the candle.

The night outside the tavern was alive. A battle host of insects chirped and clicked on all sides. Creatures—large ones, sounding larger with each passing moment—moved through the water not fifteen feet below. Birds screeched and some manner of animal screamed a death-cry in the far distance. These were the sounds that accompanied Eli into an uneasy sleep.

He awoke only a few hours later to the fact that someone was perched on the edge of his cot. He didn't move as he took a moment to assess the situation. If the intruder still believed him to be asleep—

"I know you're awake," said a woman's voice. "I heard the change in your breathing."

Never mind that plan, then.

As the woman's shape slowly clarified in the darkness, Eli glanced sideways to where his pistols still lay on the table. It probably would have been easier if she had just stolen them and gone on her way. Everything would have worked itself out in that case.

"So," he asked, "are you here to seduce me or murder me?"

The woman leaned closer, and he felt a blade against his throat. "Neither. I want to hire you."

Normally, it is quite difficult to breathe calmly with a knife at one's throat, but Eli had had some practice already. He smiled, though she likely couldn't see it. "Of course. I should have assumed. Why else would you break into my room in the middle of the night and hold a knife to my throat?"

"I figured we should get past the point where you wonder if I'm trying to kill you." She withdrew the blade. "Because if I was, I would have."

"Very comforting." There was a certain twisted logic to the approach. Sasha would have appreciated it. "If you're here to talk, can I at least know who I'm dealing with?"

The woman rose. Sparks flashed and the yellow light of the candle stub illuminated the woman from the tavern.

Her red hair hung loose, and a pair of large knives now accented her outfit. "My name is Marion."

"And what is it that you want me to do, Marion?" This was not Eli's preferred recruitment method, but it didn't change the fact that they did need a job.

"I need to find my father."

So far, so good. Eli twisted to sit on the edge of the bed and rubbed sleep from his eyes. "I see. And where would we be looking for him?"

"Here in The Green," said Marion, "but I don't know where exactly. I need you to help me track him."

"*Help* you track him?" And there was the complication. Because it was never, ever simple, was it? Commoners tended to get in the way on jobs—and besides, Sasha wouldn't like it.

Marion nodded. "No offense, but if I sent you off into The Green alone, I doubt you would come back. I've lived all my life here—hunted, tracked criminals, faced bounty hunters. The only reason I haven't gone already is that no one goes alone into the parts of The Green I suspect we'll need to travel. So far, I haven't been able to find anyone willing to go with me. You help me, and you'll be paid, but the circumstances of the job are not open to debate."

Eli rubbed at his neck. Did the tavern serve alcohol in the middle of the night? The woman standing in front of him seemed confident enough. She was rough, obviously, but a fighter like Eli had the ability to recognize a similar spirit. Marion—whoever she was—had proven herself in the past. She would not be the worst companion he had ever taken on.

"What amount of payment might we be discussing here? Our rates are—"

Marion interrupted by dropping a pouch on the table. Candlelight glinted off the edges of silver coins inside. "There's more where that came from," she said.

Eli set aside questions of where someone in The Green acquired so much money. Now it really was his decision. A simple tracking mission, partial payment upfront—if they weren't in The Green, he might already have agreed. Sasha would object—but she would object to everything until they set their sights on home. He doubted they'd receive a better offer. Eli took the pouch from the table.

Marion nodded. "We'll meet below at dawn to set a plan. We leave as soon as everything is in order."

"I think—" Eli started to say, but Marion was already closing the door behind her. He listened to her footsteps fade away before turning to blow out the candle. A large, gray spider crept across the table with its eyes fixed on him. He watched it a moment before catching it between two fingers. Hissing audibly, the thing twisted and flailed in his grip. He tossed it out the window—far out the window.

No, Sasha would not like this plan at all.

Chapter 5.
Beginnings and Discoveries

ELI EMERGED from the tavern into a truly, remarkably lovely morning. The early light was a haze of green already marked by a thickness of the air and the buzzing of blood-thirsty insects. His clothes had been damp from the moment he dressed, and now they grew heavy, clinging to his body as he walked down the street to the stable. "Good morning!"

Sasha turned to glare at him and said nothing. Eli saw the stablehand in the corner, clutching a bucket to his chest and staring at Sasha through eyes wide with exhausted fear.

A broken shelf lay on the ground and a water barrel had been overturned, but the boy appeared unharmed and the stable otherwise undamaged. "Breakfast is being prepared," he said by way of greeting. It was always best to start with food when it came to Sasha.

She held her glare for another moment before shoving past Eli and heading for the tavern. He winked at the stablehand and tossed the lad a silver piece. He made no move to catch it, and the coin landed on the boy's chest. "Buck up," Eli told him. "It's over now."

Sasha was still scowling—her ears back and her jaw clenched—when Eli caught up with her. "What's got you in such a mood?"

Her eye flashed. "Bugs, monsters, stink, quivering children—take your pick."

"I—"

Sasha cut him off. "You slept in a private room, so save it. Get me some breakfast and maybe I'll forgive you." He didn't bother pointing out that his private room was smaller than Sasha's stable and also inhabited by large insects.

Marion was waiting for them at a tall table on the far side of the tavern. She inclined her head as Eli started toward her, but Sasha stopped in the doorway. "What have you gotten us into now?"

"A job," Eli said. "That's what we wanted, right?"

"I want to go home," Sasha answered. "But as that doesn't seem likely...." She followed him to the table and the large bowl of marsh grasses set out for her. Sasha sniffed at the grass while Eli made introductions. She sampled a bite and Eli watched her chew it cautiously before taking another with greater enthusiasm.

"It's sweet grass," Marion explained. "I hope you like it."

Sasha looked at the woman with a touch more interest. "I didn't expect to find anything sweet here."

"It's just a matter of knowing where to look."

Sasha finished the contents of her bowl—which Jaylin immediately replenished before slipping away again— while Eli and Marion ate cutlets of some sort of spiny fish alongside oily slices of fruit with a tart but not unpleasant flavor.

Sasha waited until they were finished before fixing her eye on Eli again. "Now, what stupidity are we planning?"

"Sasha." He glanced at Marion. "I—"

"Don't 'Sasha' me today, Eli. I'm tired, I'm grumpy, and trekking off into The Green has an inherent stupidity to it—which I trust our employer knows, or we shouldn't be working for her to begin with—so stop being my mother and tell me what we're planning."

"Well put," said Marion.

Well put? Eli wasn't used to being outnumbered.

Well, he was, but only in more violent situations, and then he always had Sasha to back him up. In this case, he simply shrugged, leaning back in his chair. "Very well." If Marion could handle Sahsa's bluntness, maybe they all could get along.

Marion began. "Twenty years ago, my father was banished from Harman's Folly. What I—"

Eli coughed and sat up straight. "Sorry, did you say twenty years?"

Sasha flashed a smirk his way as his confidence faltered. Perhaps he should have asked just a couple more questions the night before.

"Yes."

"Do you expect him to still be—" Eli stopped himself from saying *alive*—"in the area?"

"Recently, a bounty hunter came through town. He spoke of a man deep in The Green—a man whose description matches that of my father. I've never dared venture as far as this man described—hence the reason I don't want to go alone."

In truth, The Green was the only real complication Eli foresaw—other than the very real concern that Marion's father may be long gone. Or dead. "We get the rest of our payment regardless of the outcome?"

"Rest of our payment?" asked Sasha. "Have you already accepted?"

"Marion offered us a starting payment, and we're working out the details of the job now. Don't act as though I'm keeping secrets."

"Then stop keeping secrets," Sasha retorted.

Marion held her smile in check as she watched the exchange. "How long have you two been together?"

"About six years now," Eli said.

"Six years, three months, and seventeen days," Sasha clarified. "Though sometimes it feels much longer."

Marion popped a piece of fruit into her mouth, skin and all. "To answer your question. Yes, I will pay based on the length of time you travel with me regardless of the outcome. The only other things I ask are that we leave within the hour and you tell no one what we are doing."

Eli crossed his arms. "Why the secrecy?"

"You've met the overseer?"

Eli nodded.

"She is the one who banished my father. She would not take kindly to my seeking him."

"Which raises another question," said Sasha. "Why was he banished in the first place?"

"The overseer accused him of committing crimes with magic. It was spiteful slander, but she holds power enough that no one challenged her. If I find my father, perhaps I can find a way to bring him home."

Eli turned toward Sasha. "What do you think?"

"Oh, now you want my opinion? You've basically committed us already, and death by insect swarm is as good a fate as any."

It was a more willing response than he had hoped for—not that Sasha's acceptance had ever really been in question. She would follow him anywhere—complaining the entire time, certainly, but she'd always be at his back.

"That settles it," Eli said. "We'll need time to gather supplies, but we can set out as soon as that is handled."

"The supplies are gathered already," Marion said. "I've been preparing for a while now so that I'd be ready when the opportunity arose. Unless either of you requires something specific, everything should be in order for us to depart." Marion nodded toward the pistols half-concealed beneath Eli's jacket. "You'll want different weapons. Black powder doesn't last long here."

"That won't be a problem." He wasn't ready to tell Marion more than he needed to about the unique nature of his weapons. A giant could sneeze on them and they'd still work. That was as good a test as any—though Eli would have avoided that particular test had he been given a choice.

Marion raised an eyebrow in question but didn't push the issue. "So be it. We should avoid leaving together. Go to the general store and give my name. They're expecting you and will outfit you with all the supplies you need. Everything is already paid for, and you'll attract less suspicion than I would. Follow the land-bridge north of the settlement until you come to the giant's tree. I'll be waiting for you there." With that, she rose and started toward the door.

"The giant's tree?" Eli asked.

Marion turned back. "You'll know it when you see it." And then she was gone.

Eli found Sasha watching him with disapproval.

"What?"

"Is this going to be like that time we took a contract from the Gray Lady of Ironkeep?"

Eli smirked. "The contract that she paid us incredibly well for?"

Sasha narrowed her eye at him. "The contract that involved us both being taken captive and me getting shot. Twice."

"You make it sound worse than it was."

"Easy to say when you weren't the one that got shot."

"I had to fight that brute though. What did he call himself again?"

"The Anvil. Terrible name. But that doesn't mean anything. He went down after a single blow to the head."

"I got injured."

"You took a flesh wound to the hand," Sasha corrected. "You didn't ask enough questions then, and it got us into trouble. This feels an awful lot like the same thing. You never used to be this complacent."

"Who's being complacent?" Eli dropped a couple coins on the table. "What more would you have liked me to ask?"

Sasha mumbled something he couldn't hear—meaning she didn't have an answer but was too stubborn to admit it.

"Exactly. I don't like The Green either, but this is as good a job as we're likely to find, so let's go out there and do what we're good at."

"Rush into situations we don't understand, surviving by luck and mad schemes?"

Eli adjusted his hat. "Exactly."

~ ~ ~

The general store was run by two gray-haired women identical in appearance and dress who finished each other's sentences. Eli entered alone and found the hairs on his arms rising the moment he stepped through the door.

The women nodded when he gave Marion's name and busied themselves with the order. Eli was tense as he waited between dim aisles formed from teetering shelves and crates of goods. Machetes lay atop rough lengths of rope which tangled with new trousers and boxes of imported spices. A row of woodcarvings depicted various rare creatures—dragons, centaurs, unicorns. The unicorn was slender and beautiful. Sasha would have scoffed at it.

"Would you like to purchase one?" asked the woman on the left. "They're only—"

"A copper piece each," finished the other.

"Or a wish."

"Or a favor."

He didn't care to ask what they meant by a wish or a favor. "No, thank you."

The women smiled in unison, and Eli felt a shiver run down his spine. It was then that he noticed both of them were also wearing small snake-head earrings—the mouths of each head open with fangs bared. He tried not to take it as an omen.

A shop assistant entered to announce that the order was ready outside. "Have a pleasant trip," said one of the women. Eli suspected they had switched places when he looked away.

"Thank you." He tipped his hat to the pair and ducked outside.

"You look like you just escaped a troll den," said Sasha.

Eli shook his head, not willing to say much where the women might still be able to hear. "Let's get loaded up."

He divided the supplies between Sasha's travel bags and his own backpack—sorting through the provisions and camping materials Marion had selected for them. Included with the order were a few odd devices Eli could not identify. He packed these carefully away, trusting her judgment.

"Heading into The Green?"

He looked up to find the overseer's guard—Merrick, was it?—watching from where he leaned against the corner of the storefront. From a glance at Sasha's posture, it was clear she hadn't heard him approach either.

"Figured we'd get a sense of the area," Eli said as he secured four machetes to Sasha's side. "We don't like staying idle." Was that a blowgun he had just loaded?

Merrick's expression did not grow friendlier. "Perhaps it would be better if you stayed around town. Rest and stay out of trouble—that was what you said right?"

Sasha rounded on the guard, almost impaling Eli on the metal rod he was attempting to secure to her side. "Perhaps it would be better if you minded your own business and let us be on our way," She shook herself, testing the fastenings. Satisfied, she nodded.

Eli pulled his own now-laden pack onto his shoulders. "I appreciate the concern." A little soothing to follow Sasha's sting couldn't hurt them. "We won't be going far."

The sheer amount of their supplies proclaimed the words a lie, but he didn't much care what the bodyguard thought of them. He and Sasha could hardly be the first arrivals to go galivanting off into The Green. Perhaps Merrick would consider himself lucky to be rid of them and leave it at that. The lines in his forehead deepened, but the guardsman did not argue further.

They set out, heading north, and Eli felt Merrick's eyes on his back every step of the way, even after they had passed beyond the town limits. But the guard made no move to follow.

Chapter 6.
The Pleasures of Local Wildlife

THE LAND bridge was a track of raised ground that wove between pools and bogs in a roughly northward direction. Despite the sharp, pale grasses and spongy ground, it proved a secure enough path—for the moment at least. In his regular position on Sasha's blind side, Eli listened close to every splash of water, every animal cry that rose around them.

Harman's Folly soon vanished behind a curtain of moss and trees and hanging vines. Out here, away from the fine trappings of civilization, it was even more evident how strange a place Eli had led them into. Whatever happened, this would not be as simple as one of their jobs back home.

And the jobs back home were never simple.

A pair of snakes hung by their tails from a nearby tree, golden eyes unblinking. Birds flitted in the branches above them. And then the clouds of biting insects descended. Eli waved his arms. He flipped his collar up and pulled it tight. He cursed the ancestors of the small, biting vermin which gnawed his flesh.

Sasha chuckled to herself, even though she wasn't watching him.

"What? Like you're not bothered—" Struck by a thought, Eli held his hand close to Sasha's side. The familiar pulse of her power radiated against his fingertips.

Blasted unicorn magic. She was leaving Eli to suffer alone. "Don't spend too much energy on these things," he said. "You may need it for something worse than insects."

"You're just jealous you can't do the same."

The flies were little more than specks that bit Eli's neck, climbed in his ears, delivered stinging bites every-where beneath his clothes—truly everywhere. Then there were larger flies—great jeweled monstrosities that drew blood with every bite. Eli watched winged twigs hover just out of reach and stare with six sets of eyes. Dark spiders clung to his boots and hissed when he kicked them away. He felt his flesh becoming more corrupted with each step.

"Stop, stop." He set himself rummaging through the bags of supplies.

"Hungry already?"

"There has to be something in here to keep the flies at bay," Eli said. "These people can't live like this all the time."

Every jar and package they had was labeled in either another language or some indecipherable local dialect. He put each back in its place, not daring to waste something important. He could face a few bugs until they got to Mar-ion. Of course he could.

"You've been quiet," he said to Sasha as they resumed walking.

"Please tell me you understand how uncertain our sit-uation is right now?" Sasha bit at a particularly large red fly which darted away.

"Which part?"

"Marion throws silver at us to find her father from twenty years ago. The overseer is already sniffing around. There has to be something we don't know."

"There always is. But what would you rather do? Sit in town and drink with the old codgers until the duke, maybe, forgets about us? Marion's silver is good, and this is what we do. I—"

"I know that," Sasha huffed. "I know we need work and in a cesspit like this, no job is going to look good. I just need to know that you aren't walking into this one blindly because a pretty face offered you money."

"When have I ever been led astray by a pretty face?"

Sasha lowered her ears and let the silence speak for her.

Eli flushed slightly. "Other than those times?"

Sasha snorted, and Eli reached out to pat her shoulder. "I do understand how risky this is," he said. "We'll be careful. And besides, if we're out in The Green, it makes it more difficult for anyone to track us. This is a good opportunity."

Continuing on, Eli realized that what he had taken for a small patch of land jutting from the water off to their right was actually a scaled creature at least as large as Sasha. Beady eyes blinked as they passed, but—thank the powers—it didn't seem interested in them otherwise.

"I know we had no choice but to come here," Sasha murmured after a few moments. "And I do trust you."

"Thank you, Sasha." He took a breath. It was good to hear those words from her this time, to get the reassurance that they—

"Even if you don't know what you're doing most of the time." The smirk was back on the unicorn's mouth.

"I would think—"

"Think that's the tree?" Sasha cut off Eli's retort.

Through a gap in the tree cover, Eli saw a towering trunk at least three times the height of any other around them. It was still some distance away but appeared to be directly in the path of the land bridge they followed. The tree's bark was bone white and opened to a broad canopy of dark leaves almost purple in color.

Eli sized up the largest tree he had ever seen in his life. "No. That one's not big enough. I figure we should probably keep looking."

Sasha snorted and picked up her pace, forcing Eli to jog to keep up with her. "You can make jokes when we're not threatened with being eaten alive."

~ ~ ~

Marion was waiting for them at the foot of the pale tree. In a change from before, she wore trousers with tall boots made from some sort of dark, scaled hide and a loose shirt with a vest laced over it. She carried a long jacket slung over one shoulder, and a battered cutlass hung at her waist. When they got closer, Eli also saw a variety of knives and a pair of hatchets on her person and a hand crossbow strapped to the side of her leg.

"She's got more weapons than you do," Sasha murmured as they approached.

"Anyone can strap weapons on and look impressive."

"You really think those are just for show?"

He had to admit that, no, even more so than before, Marion held herself as someone who knew how to handle the weapons she carried. It was in her stance, in the way she turned her head, ever so slightly, to monitor the environment. But Eli wasn't going to give Sasha the satisfaction of admitting what they both knew. "Let's just see what the plan is."

Marion stepped forward as they approached. "Did you have any trouble?"

"The overseer's guard questioned us as we were leaving." Eli nudged Sasha. "In hindsight, we should have told him we were going fishing."

Sasha looked unimpressed. "I don't know why I travel with you." She walked off to examine the giant's tree.

Marion looked concerned. "What sort of questions?"

"He wanted to know where we were going, seemed to suspect that he wouldn't like the answer—not that we gave him one."

"Did he mention me at all?"

"No. He didn't push us too hard about the matter, either."

Marion let out a breath. "Good. When they realize I'm not in town, the overseer will put things together quickly enough. But I don't expect Merrick to come after us. If we get everything loaded, we can be well away before they realize what we're doing."

"Loaded?"

In answer, Marion led Eli around the tree to a spot where the ground sloped down to the bank of a wide river which wound its way from the northeast to the southwest.

The gray water carried tufts of moss and the occasional branch on leisurely currents. Swarms of insects hovered over the water, the beating of their wings audible even at a distance. The rich, earthy, fetid aroma of the swamp was stronger here, and at the bottom of the slope, tethered to a low tree, was a raft.

The large raft was made simply of lashed logs still covered in bark. A low wall ran around the edge, and Eli spied a pair of poles he assumed were used to guide progress down the river. There was no sign of protection from the elements or insects. A regular pleasure vessel if Eli had ever seen one.

Marion threw a stick at a pile of rope in the corner of the raft—a pile of rope that uncurled itself and raised its head to look at them, baring fangs.

"This is all your fault," Sasha muttered in Eli's ear.

Marion threw another stick and the alarmingly large snake slid into the water and swam away.

Eli had to agree with Sasha—again—but she would be providing enough realism for both of them. "I think it looks lovely," he said. "How do we get down?"

Marion smiled and stepped onto the muddy hill. Keeping her feet under her, she slid down the slope, hopping over the wall and landing on the raft with a small flourish. She turned to the others with the challenge written on her face.

Eli straightened his jacket. "Well—that looked easy enough."

Sasha snorted. "Go ahead then."

"I will."

He adjusted the straps of his pack and tested its weight. He studied the ground and the tracks that marked Marion's path to the raft. Easy enough, indeed. Satisfied, he took a breath and stepped over the edge—

—and immediately felt his feet fly out from beneath him. With a curse, he couldn't stop the heavy pack from dragging him over backwards. Feeling his teeth snap shut from the impact, and with the warm, wet of mud seeping into his pants, he slid down the hill and came to a stop against the riverboat.

"Easy as hatching basilisks!" Sasha cackled while Marion held out a hand to help Eli to his feet. On secure footing once more, he ran his hands over his coat and the back of his legs, slopping away the thick globs of mud clinging there. A bit of mud was nothing new, but Eli didn't care for the amused pity in Marion's expression— especially this early in their venture. And Sasha was unlikely to let him forget this moment.

"Yeah, yeah." He flipped the unicorn a rude gesture. "Let's see you do better."

Sasha stopped laughing. She looked at the muddy slope that separated her from the raft, and her eye narrowed at Eli.

"Go on then," he told her, holding back laughter.

She stepped forward, tentatively placing a hoof into the slick track, followed by another. When both front feet started to slip, she hauled her weight backwards. "Come on," Eli called, enjoying himself now. He knew he'd pay for it the moment Sasha reached him, but for now—she was up there, he was down here, and it was rather amusing watching a battle unicorn struggle to slide down a muddy hill.

"You can do it," Marion said—sincere encouragement to Eli's teasing.

Sasha stepped forward again, tentatively lowering herself to the ground as she curled her legs under her. In this position—half lying down, half sprawled—she slid to where the others waited. Marion stepped back as Sasha stopped—but Eli only noticed her move behind him as Sasha hauled herself to her feet and shook the mud from her belly—spattering Eli with it in the process.

"Thank you for that," he said, spitting the bitter grit from his mouth. "I was concerned there were a few clean spots left on my clothes."

"Don't laugh at me," was all the answer she gave.

"But you laughed first—" Eli gave up. There was no use arguing where Sasha's pride was concerned. The unicorn stepped into the raft and took up position near the front.

"Get the line, would you?" Marion asked, one of the poles now in hand.

Damp, soiled, and swallowing his own pride, Eli untied the raft and stepped onboard as Marion poled them out into moving water.

Chapter 7.
People and Stories

IT FELT cooler on the water than it had on land. But then, just because one branding iron pressed to your arm is cooler than two, it doesn't make the one any more pleasant. All this to say that, as they floated along this river at the bottom of the world, Eli found himself longing for the windy mountain peaks of his childhood.

Out from between the trees, the air was not so close, but the heat and dampness of it still clung to his skin and weighed down his clothes. And the swarms of miniscule biting flies did not allow him a moment's relief. An hour into the trip, Sasha took one look at him and declared that he looked like a victim of the pox, what with his flushed skin and the smears of blood from fresh bites. In truth, the pox might have been a more pleasant fate.

When Eli removed his jacket against the heat, it was only to have the insects redouble their attacks. He could face down twenty enemies in complete silence, and these bugs made him want to scream. After a short time of watching him flail and curse, Marion lay aside her guide pole. Stooping over Eli, she ran a finger along the side of his neck.

Eli leaned away. "What are you doing?"

She sniffed her hand. "You didn't use the oil?"

"What oil?"

Marion sighed and rummaged through the packs they had brought. "The oil I purchased for us." She withdrew two large flasks. "It'll keep most of the flies away. Now take your shirt off."

Eli cursed himself for neglecting to ask this question as they got underway. Marion certainly did seem less troubled by the bugs than he did—which confirmed his earlier theory of the oil's usage. He noted carefully which flasks Marion had selected before stripping off his shirt and turning away at her instruction. The oil was cool to the touch as she lay her hands against his back, working the oil into his skin. Her fingers traced over his scars—the arrow wound in his shoulder, the knife slash low across his ribs, the raised band of flesh where a bullet had grazed his side. Marion made no comment on any of these. It felt good, and already the flies hardly bothered the areas she had covered.

Eli relaxed into Marion's touches, savoring the relief, the feel of her hands caressing his skin. Her hands moved lower on his back and his body began to respond in other ways. He stood straight, shaking his head to clear it. That wouldn't do at all.

There was laughter in Sasha's eyes as she recognized exactly what had happened. This was the trouble in traveling so long with one companion—it was damned impossible to hide anything from them.

Marion finished her application. "I trust you can manage the rest yourself?" She handed him the flask. "Unless there are parts you don't care about, I recommend you cover your entire body with that. And don't worry, I won't look." Her eyes flashed. "Too much."

"Eli's sensitive about things like that," Sasha said solemnly. "Very private."

Eli swallowed his retort. It would only encourage her.

On the other side of the raft, Marion hesitated as she laid her hands against the unicorn's side, no doubt caught off-guard by the power radiating from Sasha. "Don't worry," Sasha said, "It's just to keep the flies at bay. I won't hurt you."

Marion nodded and set to work with the oil. "What sort of… power is it?"

"It's rather like a ward. I can deflect attacks, lessen injury, push against things nearby."

"Do all your kind have that ability?" She sounded hesitant to ask the question. It was a familiar response. Unicorns intimidated people—especially those who had never met one before.

Eli waited, listening to how Sasha would respond. "Most do," the unicorn answered after a slight pause. "Though some train with the inborn magic more than others. I've found it to be quite useful, especially with Eli's ability to attract trouble. Though, as you can tell—" Marion's hands traced over the unicorn's scars— "it's not always enough."

"You're alive," Marion pointed out. "In these parts, that's all you need."

Once he was certain that Marion's attention was elsewhere, Eli turned his focus to the rest of his body. The oil was a cool salve to his angry skin and left a faint scent of mint in his nostrils. He quietly thanked all the powers for whoever had first discovered this oil. Even with her gone, he could almost feel Marion's fingers still gliding over his skin. Her hands were rough and calloused—like his—but her touch was gentle and—

No, no, no. This was no time for thoughts like that. He adjusted his clothes back into place and closed the jar of oil. "How long have you lived in this area?" he asked Marion.

She gave him an assessing look before answering. "I was born here. That's as much of a story as most of us have."

"Everyone has a story," Eli said. "Some just haven't learned to tell it yet." And most were more interesting than people assumed if told right.

Except for that baker back in... whatever town that was. That man would have made a minotaur attack boring just by being there.

Marion considered his statement as she returned to work. "I'm not so sure about that."

"What happened to your mother?" Sasha asked.

"We don't speak." Marion crouched down to work on Sasha's legs without elaborating.

"Why not leave then?" the unicorn pressed. "You clearly have money. Why stay in The Green if there's no one to hold you here?"

"It's the only life I've known." Marion paused from rubbing Sasha for a moment. "I've thought about leaving, certainly, but the world outside The Green has never been more than a bedtime story. What place would I have in it?"

"So, you're what—a bounty hunter?" Eli returned to his seat at the edge of the raft. The occasional fly still bit at him, but he basked in the reprieve the oil provided. He had begun to think he would be drained of blood before the end of the first day.

"Nothing so formal," Marion said. "I've chased down bounties, sure. And they've paid well enough that I can hold onto most of the silver it's brought me. But I also hunt. I've served as a guide—whatever keeps food on the table, keeps me from needing to depend on the favor of others. A little silver goes a long way here and some jobs pay handsomely."

Eli dipped his hand into the river, enjoying the cool water running between his fingers. As Marion continued oiling Sasha, the unicorn turned her attention to Eli. He saw the intent in her expression—she wanted him to press for information. *Not yet,* he answered with his look. *We still have time.* Every conversation didn't have to become an interrogation. Every person they met wasn't inherently a threat.

Sasha snorted and turned her good eye to Marion. "I have another question about your father—"

Marion cut her off when she noticed Eli's hand in the water. "You don't want to do that."

He pulled his arm back. "Why—"

The words caught in his throat. His hand had only been submerged a matter of moments, but when he withdrew it, he found a pair of large, black leeches hanging there.

"Petur's poxy arse!" Eli leapt to his feet, trying on instinct to shake the creatures free. They flapped around, slapping against the back of his hand like raw sausages—living, biting, disgusting raw sausages. Whatever he did, they remained firmly attached. He had dealt with leeches before, but—by the pox, what sort of demon worms were these?

"Calm down." Marion grabbed hold of his arm and pulled a knife from her belt. On instinct, Sasha stepped forward and Eli grabbed her knife hilt with his free hand. Marion stilled, her voice soft. "I'm not going to hurt you." She waited for him to respond.

Eli looked at the leeches—one of them giving another wet pulse against his skin—and relaxed. "Sorry." He let go of her weapon. "Old habits."

Marion lay the blade nearly flat against his skin, working it against the head of the first leech. With precise movements, she scraped it off and flung it into the river before doing the same with the second.

Eli pressed against the twin streams of blood that ran from the back of his hand. With each beat of his heart, the blood pulsed again, running over his fingers and dripping onto the raft.

"It's going to be like that for a while," Marion told him. She went back to the baggage and returned with water, a tin of salve, and bandages. It didn't take long for her to tend the twin wounds before fastening the bandages into place.

"Did we learn our lesson about the water?" Sasha asked as if he were a child. Eli stuck his tongue out at her in reply.

"Be happy," Marion said as she put the supplies away. "There are creatures in this river that could strip the flesh from your hand or take the entire arm."

"I'll keep that in mind." Eli rubbed at the bandages. He couldn't feel anything from the bites, but blood was already soaking through the cloth. Marion returned to the back of the raft and picked up the pole again.

Glancing at the water with renewed distrust, Eli went to sit with Sasha near the center of the raft. "See," he told her, "this place is lovely."

Chapter 8.
Strange Bedfellows

THEY DRAGGED the raft ashore that night on a patch of dry ground—dry, in this case, meaning they didn't sink up to their ankles with every step. Marion sorted through the supplies while Eli gathered deadwood for a fire. "We'll want it," Marion said, "to keep away visitors."

"Won't the light draw things in?" he asked her.

"It will." Marion's grin was disconcerting. "But that's still better than what would find you in the dark."

Sasha nickered. "Lovely."

While Marion was busy with the supplies, Sasha joined Eli as he began to make the fire. "Any time you want to step up now would be great," she said.

"What's that supposed to mean?" he kept his voice light but really didn't feel like having this conversation. Thankfully, Marion was safely out of earshot.

"Do you remember when that scholar hired us to protect his caravan, and you drove him to drink because of how much you questioned his decisions?"

Eli sighed. "Yes. The man couldn't navigate if he had one end of a string tied to his wrist and the other to his destination. Marion is clearly more competent of a guide, so what is your point?"

"My point," Sasha said through gritted teeth, "is that I want to see some of your obnoxious side again. Ask questions, take charge—do something. It's your responsibility, *Captain*. I imagine this swamp already has enough skeletons of scrawny humans who didn't ask enough questions."

Eli stood and met Sasha's eye. "I'm not a captain here. It's Marion's expedition, her territory. We're here to shoot things that get too bold and get her home in one piece."

"There's more to this," Sasha fired back. "And when it comes into play, we're going to want some warning."

Eli knelt back to the firewood, arranging it so it would burn better. Sasha wasn't wrong, as usual. "I get the sense that pushing her won't get us anywhere," he answered. It wasn't the full truth, but it would have to do for now. "We keep watch; no one gets hurt. Anything more than that, we'll figure out in time."

Eli would figure it out—though, beyond the niggling cloud at the back of his thoughts, he wasn't certain what he was trying to work out just yet.

Sasha huffed, but didn't push him further. Instead, she watched as he tried a few strikes of the flint. Sparks flared and faded, refusing to catch in the damp shavings. "You need help with that?"

"I can handle it," he muttered. "I just—" His next attempt barely counted as sparks.

"Looks like a farting pixie," Sasha said.

Before Eli could argue, Marion crouched beside him and took the flint and steel for herself. "I'll get that."

He rose to get out of the way, and before he could see how she did it, young flames had begun to crackle merrily at the base of the wood.

Marion adjusted the logs as the flames climbed higher. "Don't worry," she said, "it comes with experience.

The wood here doesn't like to cooperate. Now, I'm going to catch a few fish for dinner. Will you two mind the fire?"

"Of course."

Eli felt Sasha watching him as Marion walked off, heard the mockery in her silence. "Don't say anything," he muttered.

"You hate this," Sasha chuckled. "You feel like a beardless recruit all over again—insect bites, trouble with the fire, Marion's providing the food and rubbing you down with oils. You feel helpless."

"I don't see you helping out."

"My job is taking orders," Sasha said. "And so far, my *captain*,"—the word was barbed in her mouth—"hasn't given any. At all."

Eli waved her off. "You want an order, go keep watch or something." Sasha snorted and watched him untie the bandages on his hand. Hours later, and the twin bites were still bleeding freely.

"Remind me to never go in the water," Sasha said.

~ ~ ~

They dined on lumpy river fish supplemented with provisions from the packs. Marion helped Sasha identify which marsh grasses were worth eating, and the unicorn spent much of her time grazing before going to sleep.

At least when she was eating, she wasn't trying to tell him what to do.

After setting aside a comfortable supply of wood, Marion tossed a handful of pungent powder into the fire. "It'll keep the insects at bay," she explained, settling in to take the first watch.

The scent made his eyes water and reminded Eli of a back-alley meat seller he and Sasha had met once. He hadn't asked what sort of meat the woman sold.

Eli had learned the talent of sleeping anywhere with little difficulty, but the dreams that came to him the first night were dark and unsettled. Things seemed to move in the darkness just out of sight as colors and strange aethers flared and faded away.

From the darkness—it was still a dream, no?—he saw Marion lie down beside him. With a smile, she caressed one hand up his leg, sliding it along his thigh. Her touch was warm, firm. The hand inched higher.

But something was not right. The very real touch against his body dragged him back to wakefulness, and Eli's reflexes flared to life at the sight of the six-foot snake curling its way up his leg.

He cursed—creatively—but forced himself not to startle the creature more than he already had. It was mottled black and heavy as its head crept up his chest. Closer to his face, it opened its mouth in a quiet hiss to reveal rows of pointed fangs. His pistols were nearby but reaching for them would only provoke the animal currently making itself familiar with Eli's most sensitive places.

"Marion," he hissed over the sound of his own pounding heart. "Marion."

She twisted around to see what the trouble was. "Oh."

She didn't sound nearly concerned enough for Eli's liking. Neither did she immediately do anything about the vicious beast which was at this point very nearly crawling down his throat. Its tongue flicked against his nose as the black head swayed across his vision.

"I haven't seen one of them in years," Marion continued—whispering at least, but that was about all the help she was providing. "We call them specters on account of the way they catch people unawares so easily."

If he had been far, far away from here, in front of a roaring fire, with a nice cup of mulled wine in hand—Eli might have been interested to hear what the creature was called. Now, however, he focused all his efforts on breathing even slower than he already was.

"Maybe," he said through gritted teeth, "you just weren't paying close enough attention." His eyes didn't leave the black beads watching him from the snake's head.

"You're fine," Marion chided. "Just don't move." She drew a hatchet from her belt.

Eli had concerns about this course of action. However, Marion offered him no chance to voice them before she swung the weapon.

With a single smooth motion, she caught the snake just behind the skull, slicing upward through its neck and severing the head in a spray of blood. Eli scrambled backwards, kicking the twitching thing off himself.

"I—" he pushed to his feet and brushed himself off, "do not like snakes."

Marion picked up the now-headless body. "You're welcome. Now help me string it up outside of camp. Then it's your watch."

"What's all the noise?" mumbled Sasha, raising her head from where she had been sleeping.

"Nothing," Eli told her, wiping blood from his face. She wasted no time in going back to sleep.

Eli stared at the snake's severed head a short distance away. The head stared back. He showed it what he thought of its defiance by kicking it into the darkness beyond their camp.

With practiced motions, their employer wrapped the snake in some sort of oil-cloth treated to mask the smell from other predators, and Eli helped her hang it from a branch for the night. Then she left him to take the second watch.

He watched as she curled into her bedroll and didn't move again. No doubt she was withholding information from them about this whole adventure—but he also trusted that she didn't mean them harm. He was good enough—usually—at reading people to have faith in that assessment.

Part of what Eli hadn't admitted to Sasha was that he was simply tired of trying to unravel plots and intrigue every time they took a job. This was how it used to be, years ago—someone else who knew what they were doing was in charge. That person gave orders, and Eli followed them. He had walked away from that life for his own reasons, and he didn't regret it. But still, it was a pleasant rest to let someone else lead the way for a while—even if it wouldn't last.

In the meantime, he no longer had any doubts about Marion's ability to handle her weapons.

Chapter 9.
The Joy of Making Friends

ELI'S HAND had stopped bleeding by the time they set out the following morning. Marion put more salve on the bites just to be safe but confirmed that there appeared to be no reason for concern.

"Like swamp decay," she said when he asked what sort of problems could occur.

He wished he could withdraw the question.

Sasha was in better spirits this morning. "Hey, Eli," she asked as Marion pushed their raft back out into the river. "Feel like a nice swim?"

While the others appeared to have benefitted from the rest, Eli's head was still in a cloud. Too tired to banter, he offered a weak rude gesture in reply and took the guide-pole from Marion when she asked him to.

"Don't hit anything; don't sink us," she said by way of instruction. "Simple enough, right?"

He hoped that would indeed be the case. When Marion produced the same book he had seen her reading in the Folly, he couldn't help but try to see what it was. She smirked when she noticed him craning his neck in an effort to glimpse the cover.

"It's volume four of the adventurers of Odan the wanderer," she told him.

That was disappointing. "Why would you read that?" Eli asked.

Marion frowned at him. "Did you see a lot of reading options in the Folly?"

Eli had to admit that he hadn't. Books didn't seem to be one of their priorities. "But Odan?" he asked. "He's the worst liar I've ever met."

Marion sat up straighter. "You've met him?"

The excitement on her face couldn't be allowed to last—not in this case.

"I have. He's a two-timing penny-pincher who takes money from old women."

Sasha took the opening to insert herself into their conversation. "Eli's bitter because Odan beat him at cards. Badly."

"He was cheating!" Eli was sure of it.

Marion waved him off. "If that's how you're going to be, just let me enjoy my reading. You mind the raft. We're drifting off course."

And so they were. Eli spent the next ten minutes adjusting them back to the center of the current, and when things were settled, Marion was again engrossed in the pages of her book of lies. Well, if she wanted to be misled, that was her choice.

Thankfully—so long as he paid attention—managing the raft wasn't so difficult as Eli might have feared. The current did most of the work, and Sasha declared her amazement when they stopped at noon that he hadn't run them aground. They ate, reapplied the oil to their skin, and continued on their way.

With Marion humming to herself at the back of the raft, and Sasha dozing in the middle, Eli claimed the front and watched the landscape pass them by—though he was

careful not to allow any parts of his body too close to the water.

The river was wider here. With the added space, the air was less close—though a merciless sunlight filled any gap left in the oppressive humidity. He pulled the wide brim of his hat lower and leaned against one of their packs as he looked for motion among the trees. Lizards and birds scurried from one branch to the next. Closer by, large creatures watched their passage—beady eyes poking above submerged bodies.

A flutter of movement drew Eli's attention to a large, gray bird perched on a fallen tree. It gave a three-note call and fanned its tail—long feathers flaring out in a half-circle composed of bright orange spotted with red and gold, trimmed with black. Amidst so many things that wanted to eat Eli—and make his life miserable if they couldn't, it was something truly beautiful. It called again, its head turning to mark their progress, before lowering its feathers and darting into the underbrush.

Eli let himself drift toward sleep. He pulled his hat low and rolled up his shirt sleeves to avail himself of the pittance of breeze that drifted past. Time passed to the sound of Marion's low melody and the slap of water against the sides of the raft. Something splashed nearby. More bird calls sounded in the reaches of The Green. An insect—something large and probably unpleasant—buzzed nearby. For a moment at least, perhaps this wasn't such a terrible place after all.

The insect buzzed closer, passing Eli's head before circling back to hover near his face. He swatted at the thing, but it avoided him. Grudgingly, he lifted his hat from his eyes.

It was not an insect that hovered there, staring into his face from a hand's breadth away. The creature's naked flesh was a pale color that mixed shades of green and pink. Its knobby skin glowed with a faint shimmer, and from its back, translucent wings vibrated with a buzzing insect hum. When it saw he was awake, the creature grinned with pointed teeth and eagerly waved one spindly hand in greeting.

Then it bit him on the nose.

With a yell, Eli straightened, swiping at the thing which darted away to hide behind Marion. He heard her low laugh as the thing buzzed and chirped in her ear.

"What is that?" Eli asked, checking his nose for blood. Had he thought it was pleasant here? Perilous, was certainly what he meant. Painful. A clear predicament.

Marion wasn't trying very hard to hold back her amusement. "It's a faerie obviously."

"I've met faeries," Eli told her. "They don't look like that. And they may not be known for their manners, but I've never had one bite me." Yes, he was definitely bleeding. And—by the pox—that bite stung!

"Maybe that's true of northern faeries," Marion said. "But southern faeries are a whole different breed—and they'll make for excellent friends if you treat them with respect."

"It bit me," he repeated, emphasizing each word. Obviously, she had misheard him the first time.

Sasha chuckled. "Serves you right for all those jokes you made when we arrived about how much you love The Green."

"I should warn you," Marion said. "Their bites are slightly venomous—though nothing to be concerned about."

Eli swore, enough to make Sasha raise her eyebrows at him. It was an expression that never looked quite natural on her.

Was everything in this place out to harm him? Eli met Marion's unconcerned gaze. "What's it doing here?"

Marion made some sort of chirping sound which coaxed the faerie to perch on her shoulder. "It's just here to talk," she said. "If we're nice, maybe we'll learn something useful."

Eli sat down again, turning his back on Marion and her new friend.

"Aw," Sasha coddled. "Did the wee little faerie hurt you?"

"Shut up." He pulled the nearest pack closer and leaned against it, tugging his hat over his eyes and listening to the poxy thing chatter away in Marion's ear.

~ ~ ~

Eli woke from his nap somewhat more refreshed but annoyed to find the faerie still present—now sitting on Sasha's back and eating a large berry in great, juicy bites. The previous night's lack of sleep, combined with his body's general discomfort, had made him irritable. He didn't like being irritable, so he took a slow breath to center himself before standing and stretching the stiffness from his back. Maybe they all simply got off to a bad start?

"It's still here?" he asked, trying to maintain a neutral tone.

The faerie waved at him, flashing its toothy grin before chirping something that made Marion smile.

Eli wasn't sure he wanted to know. "What is it?"

"The faerie would like you to know its name is Gnit the noble," Marion translated.

"No, it isn't."

When the sunlight glinted off those venomous, pointed teeth, even a smile looked sinister. Sasha grinned as well, though she had the decency to try and hide it—as much as she ever concealed her amusement when it was at Eli's expense.

Marion shrugged. "I'm just the translator. But remember, faeries always make better friends than enemies."

Eli groaned. "Very well. Gnit the noble it is." The little beast just about beamed at him.

"Gnit has promised to talk to the other faeries," Marion explained. "They will let us know if they discover anything related to our search. In the meantime, we'll be stopping at a nearby settlement. They may be able to help us, and it will be a safe place to rest and resupply before the next leg of our journey."

"You've been this far before?" Sasha asked.

"Of course." Marion adjusted their course slightly. "I've traveled much of this river."

"Yet you never searched for your father before now?" The unicorn pressed. "Never asked about him at this settlement we're headed to?"

"I was eight when he left," Marion said. "At first, no one would tell me anything. Once I was old enough to investigate on my own, I had every reason to believe my father was long gone—until recently. The information I received points us south—away from the river and into areas I've never traveled. From the settlement, we'll be going on foot."

Eli considered the creatures they had encountered already. "What do you know of the southern regions?"

"They are less inhabited—by humans, that is—but otherwise should not be so different from what we have encountered thus far." Marion said. "With a little caution, I don't foresee any new problems. I trust that a mercenary such as yourself is not scared to venture into the untraveled reaches of The Green for fear of insects."

Was that really who Eli had become in her eyes—the worrying grandmother of their expedition? He looked at Sasha and saw her laughing at him. "I look forward to it," he told them both, filling his voice with all the confidence he could muster. "Lead on."

Chapter 10.
Another Mild Inconvenience

ELI HAD grown accustomed to jobs being unpredictable. His commanders in the northern military had drilled it into them—sometimes through very… memorable means.

You wake up with twenty snakes dumped on your head even once, and you learn to react quickly to surprises.

But even more than the unexpected, the early part of Eli's life had been defined by orders he didn't always understand. And—whether through complex decisions, miscommunication, or simple ignorance—those orders could change rapidly. He had learned to adjust—and keep his people alive in the process.

Mercenary work was much the same. From the beginning, he had been selective in the jobs he accepted. But even his best attempts to weed out the bad jobs were imperfect. There was the time he and Sasha had been hired to track down an earl's escaped prize stallion—and found the animal tied at the center of a bandit camp. Or the time they had escorted a viscount's son on a pilgrimage—without being told that the charming young lad had a gang of brutes chasing him, intent on delivering a well-earned beating.

Yes, Eli was used to surprises, and had become adept at responding to them. But the fact remained that on occasion, life still managed to well and truly catch him off guard.

The arrival of a man swinging from the tree line to snatch him from the raft was one such occasion.

Eli was standing near the front of the raft when it happened. He noticed movement in the branches on the nearby riverbank, heard the sound of something coming toward him, and began to turn. He had a hand on one of his pistols when a strong grip wrapped around his waist and Eli found himself not standing on... well, anything.

Amidst the blur of movement and the sensation of the raft disappearing from beneath him, he recognized that he had been seized by a man in ragged clothes who stank of swamp and unwashed flesh—and that this man was swinging on a rope attached to the canopy which hung low and close over this part of the river. Before he could form a suitable response to this truly irritating development, the man released him, sending him plunging toward the opposite riverbank.

Eli landed in a roll, tumbling into a pool of stagnant water and coming up on one knee, battle ready. He gripped his pistols in their holsters and cast his eyes over his surroundings. There were three people waiting for him—each with a crossbow aimed at his chest. The fourth arrived a moment later with a broad knife clutched in his hand.

Three men, one almost too old to be a bandit any longer. One girl with a shaved head whose snarl was nearly animal. She was the only one Eli felt any real concern about—other than the threat of crossbow bolts to the chest of course. Those tended to hurt regardless of who pulled the trigger. But their gear, their handling of the weapons, the slight hesitation in their demeanors—these were not murderous thieves. Hunters, was Eli's best guess.

Opportunists. Like spooked kittens, best treated with a gentle hand if at all possible.

Eli did not draw his weapons just yet. Slowly, he removed his hands from inside his jacket and spit out the mouthful of mud he had gained from his fall. Something moved in the muck beneath his knee as water soaked through his pants and ran into his boot. Watching for sudden movement, he wiped his face and hoped that whatever creature he was kneeling on didn't have fangs.

The man at the center of the group edged forward. The leader, then. "We'll be relieving you of those pistols there," he said.

Eli groaned. At least they weren't just trying to kill him. But it might have been easier if they had. "Now? You're going to make me deal with this now?"

Of course, it was the pistols. It was always the pistols.

The bandit frowned, confusion flitting across his face. Eli stood, and when the movement didn't get him killed, he continued. "Do you think you're the first ones to try and take these from me? Listen, I'm busy. I was finally dry. I just got these clothes clean—at least, as clean as I can get anything around here. Honestly, this is the worst timing."

Eli really didn't feel like killing anyone today—regardless of how much they were delaying him.

"Eli!" Sasha's shout came from further down the river, beyond the thick growth of the swamp. She would be arriving in a few moments and make the entire situation much more violent. He wasn't the only one who had heard her. A couple of the bandits glanced back that way.

Eli also didn't like the idea of getting shot again—not if he could avoid it.

"We're in the middle of The Green," he said, drawing the bandits' attention back to himself. "How did you even know I have pistols?"

When the man who had grabbed him grinned, Eli looked closer. The crooked smile, the half-missing nose—"You were in the Folly, playing cards that evening." He didn't need the man to confirm. Bandit scouts marking fresh travelers was a common enough tactic.

Sasha was getting closer. She forced her way through the undergrowth with characteristic subtlety—almost none. He had to deal with this quickly. Plus, the old man's arms were starting to shake. Eli didn't need him firing by accident. "You don't want these pistols anyway," he told them. "They're cursed. It won't end well for you. It's in all of our best interests that you just let me go back to my companions before anyone gets hurt. What do you say?'

In answer, the three with the crossbows tightened their grips on the weapons, fingers on the triggers. Eli was counting down in his head now to the moment when Sasha would burst through the wall of greenery just behind the group as likely to kill him by accident as with intention.

There was no more time to waste. "As you will." He slowly withdrew the pistols.

Excitement glinted in the leader's eyes. It was always about the money. "Toss 'em here."

Eli complied, resigned to simply getting the exchange over with. What were the chances he could find a good drink all the way out here?

The man with the knife snatched the pistols from the mud. "Pleasure doing business with you." He grunted at his cohort, and the four vanished into the swamp. The girl waved a final goodbye as she left.

Eli sighed and brushed more of the muck from his clothes. Just one, he wished—one job without some thick-headed, poxy fool complicating all of Eli's plans. Was that such an unreasonable thing to hope for?

A moment later, Sasha crashed through the undergrowth. "Where are they?"

"Gone." Eli straightened his coat and brushed past Sasha to follow her track back to the raft. He didn't need her trying to hunt them down right now.

"What do you mean, gone?"

"I mean they're gone," Eli repeated. "They took my pistols and left. It wasn't about us. One of them spotted the guns in town, and they're probably going to try and make some silver pawning them to the next unhappy traveler who comes through here with coin. They'd be worth enough even if they were just regular guns."

"They *took* your pistols?" Sasha asked—the accusation clear.

This was another conversation Eli really did not want to have again. "Well, I gave them up rather than take a crossbow bolt to the face."

"How many were there?"

"Four."

"Eli," Sasha said. "You can take four bandits, twice that on a good day."

But apparently, they were having it anyway. "I've told you, I'm tired of fighting. I'm tired of dealing with bandits and mercenaries and bounty hunters all ready to draw a weapon at a moment's provocation. I'm tired of nobles and slavers and ornery grandmothers with large needles." Sasha bit back a laugh. "Those pistols always bring trouble. If I actually thought I was rid of them, I'd be a happy man."

"The Eli who saved my life years ago was a soldier who didn't back down from a fight," Sasha said.

He turned to face her. "Sasha, don't you ever get tired of fighting?"

"No." The answer was immediate. "I was born for this life. And the world needs fighters, especially in places like this. You still believe that, or else you would have hung up your weapons long ago and settled down in a little cottage to grow vegetables and tell stories to children."

"I did, remember?"

"Yeah, that lasted how long?"

He didn't bother answering. They emerged from the trees to find Marion waiting beside the raft, her weapons at the ready. "What happened?"

"They took my pistols," Eli said.

"He gave them his pistols." Sasha corrected.

Marion looked shocked. "You just gave them up?"

"They'll be back."

"The bandits?" Marion waited for explanation, but Eli was already stepping back onto the raft.

"No, they're gone." He wasn't making things clearer. "It doesn't matter. We have other weapons."

Onboard, he fitted himself with a rapier and a hand crossbow like the one Marion carried. Meanwhile, Marion untied the raft and pushed them back into the current. "You certainly have a knack for attracting trouble," she said.

If only she knew how true that statement was. "It's the unfortunate consequence of traveling with a unicorn and a pair of unique weapons. They tend to attract unwelcome attention."

Sasha interrupted. "Really, it's just because Eli can't keep his head down."

He rose to her baiting and flashed a grin. "Remember that time your snoring gave us away to the escaped criminals we were tracking?"

"No," Sasha said, glaring back, "I don't."

One point for Eli.

Without another word, Sasha lay down and fell asleep.

Chapter 11.
Stories by Firelight

ELI KEPT watch for signs of the settlement Marion had claimed they would soon reach. They had agreed to keep traveling through twilight rather than pass another night in the open, and as the shadows broadened and shifted into darkness, he saw the first torches glimmering on the riverbank above them. At first, they passed only scattered huts, then larger bungalows connected by bridges and with wooden stairs leading down to the water's edge. The buildings were overgrown with vines and moss—nearly part of the landscape around them. When he turned his head, it seemed as though the structures at the edge of his vision faded away. What must it be like, he wondered, to live in a place like this, surrounded by such fierce wilderness, so cut off from everywhere else in the world?

Three people waited for them at a curve of the river where the current slowed. Marion hailed the strangers, tossing the line to the nearest, who caught it and hauled the raft to shore. As they drew near the greeting party, Eli realized it was not only the strange light of the swamp that colored their skin with a faint green hue.

The strangers were not so old as Eli had first assumed. Rather, their skin was weathered and rough, alternately sagging and clinging to the bones beneath. Combined with their unusual skin tone, it gave their flesh a bark-like appearance. Like their dwellings, they were nearly part of The Green itself. Adding further to this image was the mossy lichen growing on the sides of their faces, along their arms, across their bare feet. Where the lichen grew, dark veins spread beneath the skin. As the raft bumped against the shore, Eli saw that the growth had reached one of the women's eyes, stretching tendrils across the now-milky surface.

Marion smiled at them in greeting, stepping off the raft to clasp the outstretched arm of the woman at the front of the group. They exchanged quiet words in a tongue Eli could not understand while Sasha shifted closer to his side.

"Eli," murmured the unicorn, "this is strange."

"Indeed." He saw more people moving amidst the bungalows on the rise above them. Some of the houses were set on the land; others perched on stilts or clung to tree branches. Those people he caught glimpses of all bore the marks of the lichen somewhere on their bodies. Whatever else Eli had to say about the Green, this adventure would make a fine story someday.

"Come," said Marion, turning back to them. "We will stay here tonight. And tomorrow, they will help us on our way with guidance and provisions." With that, Marion followed the three strangers up the slope toward the nearest bungalow.

"You go ahead," said Sasha. "I'm sleeping right here where I'm not going to breathe until we're well away from this place. I don't need whatever-that-is growing all over me."

"Come on." He patted Sasha's shoulder before he stepped ashore and followed Marion. "Whatever this is, we'll face it together." He heard Sasha's groan before she followed him up the hill.

~ ~ ~

Inside the largest bungalow, Marion introduced Zeti and Zoti who she explained were the elders, shamans, and advisors of this particular settlement. The pair were older—with hair that was going white, few teeth, and lichen covering more of their bodies than it left bare. The couple sat before a low table spread with food and illuminated by tallow candles which flickered with uneasy light. A few children stood near the door, apparently ready to serve, and Eli spied other curious eyes peeking in at the windows as he offered his name and sat beside Marion. He kept himself attuned to the surroundings, listening for danger, but Marion appeared at ease in this place. That, at least, was reassuring.

Zeti spoke first. "We welcome you to our home." The old man's words were thick and came slowly, but Eli heard sincerity behind them.

"Indeed," said Zoti, her braids swaying with every movement of her head, "there are not many who make the journey to our village, and fewer still who stay to trade words or stories."

Eli glanced as Sasha, ready for some snide comment about his storytelling, but the unicorn was silent—turning her head side-to-side to watch the room with one uneasy eye.

"There will be time for words soon," said Zeti. "First, let us eat."

The meal caught Eli by surprise. Their hosts served more of the spiny fish that seemed common to the region, but this time covered in a berry jam which flavored the dish with a sweet tang unlike anything he had tasted before. They ate this alongside hunks of snake, roasted bird and roots fried in oil, strange pale fruits that burst when Eli bit them, and raw tentacles wrapped in grass that he found himself enjoying despite all his best intentions. There were pitchers full of cool, clear water, and others which held a pale, green wine that was sweet and strong and tingled as he swallowed it.

They provided Sasha with a bale of the sweet grass she had developed a taste for, as well as roots and fruit from the table. The meal passed mostly in silence, though Marion occasionally traded a comment and a laugh with their hosts in the other language. Whatever Eli had expected to find here—it hadn't been comfort and laughter and food to rival the best northern kitchens.

The animals outside continued their never-ending chorus, and as the last remnants of the meal were cleared away, Eli heard someone in a nearby bungalow begin playing a woodwind instrument of unfamiliar tone. A drum soon added its low timbre to the simple melody, then a woman's voice began to sing words he could not translate—but that he felt he perhaps understood nonetheless.

Zeti poured another round of wine, even providing some in a bowl for Sasha who offered her appreciation. "Now," said Zoti, "let us share words with one another." The couple looked at each of them in turn, but Eli waited, allowing Marion to explain their quest as she would.

"I am looking for my father," Marion said. "He was banished from my village years ago, but recently, I have heard that he may still be living somewhere in The Green."

"What have you heard?" asked Zoti.

"A visitor who passed through said he saw a man watching him in the deep south, a man who leaned on a wooden staff."

Eli glanced at Sasha, who was staring at him in accusation. He looked away before she could read the thoughts on his face. If that brief sighting was all that fueled their investigation, then finding Marion's father was a tenuous hope at best. And if Eli had asked more questions at the start, they would have known this—exactly as Sasha had warned him.

Marion continued. "I believe this man may be my father, and I want to ask you, respected elders, if you have any information that might help in my search."

Zeti and Zoti traded looks with each other. "We also have heard stories of this man," Zeti said.

Eli straightened, and Sasha's accusation faded to the background. When the elders did not explain further, Marion leaned forward, her plea written across her face. "What sort of stories? Please, any information could prove useful."

"Not much is certain," said Zoti. "It is said that he lives in a part of The Green where few travel, and from which even fewer return."

"We call it *tempar gap*—the dark place." Zeti made a sign to ward away evil.

"I have faced the dangers of The Green before," Marion said.

Zoti shook her head. "The beasts in *tempar gap* are not like those that roam other places in the world. They are grown fierce, and their blood mingles with the dark aethers of the swamp, changing them. Horrors live beneath those waters, alongside other, stranger things—specters and wraiths that are not of this world."

"If I may," Eli said. The eyes of the elders turned on him in mirrored movements. "I have encountered other such places in the north—forsaken areas long abandoned, the legends of which are soon grown beyond truth. I do not doubt that there are dangers to the south, but if a man can live there alone for years, the three of us can journey there and back to speak with him."

"Only a dark wizard could survive so long in such a place," said Zeti. "Perhaps it is even his power that taints the area in such a way."

"My father is not a dark wizard!" Marion's knuckles turned white as she gripped her cup. She took a calming breath. "My father was always skilled at navigating The Green, nothing more. As my companion has observed, some stories grow beyond reality."

"They are more than stories." Zeti held up his arm. By the light of the candles, beneath the lichen that grew thick in places, Eli saw thick bands of scar tissue that ran from elbow to wrist. "I have met the creatures of *tempar gap*," the elder said. "They are as real as you or I."

"Though," Zoti continued the thought with slight hesitation. "It may be that we do not know the whole truth. Perhaps the man we have heard of is your father, and perhaps he is indeed the man you believe him to be. It is not for us to say."

"We will find the truth," Marion said. "All we ask is your direction to this place—as well as shelter for the night and supplies for our journey. We have money and goods to offer in exchange."

Zeti and Zoti looked at each other again, sharing thoughts in some way beyond Eli's perception. He was never entirely comfortable around people who didn't need to speak in order to understand each other.

Sasha's glare was still boring into the side of his head as the elders held silent conference. He grudgingly looked back at her. *Not a word*, he thought intently at her.

She rolled her eye and went back to her bowl of wine.

Apparently reaching some sort of decision, the two elders nodded. "We will help you," Zoti affirmed. "But you must accept our help with a warning—do not assume you know what awaits you in *tempar gap*."

"We will prepare for any danger," Marion said, "but of this much I am certain—my father is innocent, and I intend to prove it."

Zeti and Zoti said nothing more.

Well, Eli thought, at least they were keeping up tradition—no boring, simple jobs for Eli and Sasha! He might almost have been disappointed if things had gone entirely to plan.

Almost.

~ ~ ~

After the meeting finished, people curious to meet the newly arrived strangers filled the bungalow. And while they showed Sasha a level of awed deference, Eli received no such concern.

"What are they saying?" he asked as a dozen children surrounded him, tugging at his coat and rummaging through his pockets.

"They want to know your name," Marion translated as Eli fought to keep his possessions close. "And where you are from, why you are here, where you are going, if you have ever been in a fight, or met a king, or seen a dragon?"

"Is that all?" He snatched one of his knives back from a tall boy he hadn't noticed standing behind him.

Marion did not seem inclined to help him escape his current situation. "All I understood. I still have difficulties with the language and... well, there are quite a lot of them."

"So I noticed." He had to raise his voice to be heard over the clamor of young voices. He tucked his coin purse out of sight and pulled his coat tighter, failing to disentangle himself from the horde. Marion laughed at him and crossed the room to join a couple women who greeted her warmly.

The bungalow continued to fill with the sounds of merrymaking. The instruments Eli had heard earlier made an appearance, now joined by a few others. The melody remained low—not at all the jigs and reels of northern taverns—but there was an ethereal beauty to the sound as it mingled with the multitude of voices and the noises of the world outside.

There was more food, more wine, and the older villagers began smoking some sort of leaf which gave off a sweet, pungent aroma and hovered in a cloud just over their heads. At Eli's count, there were maybe thirty adults and half as many children present. Few of the adults attempted to speak with him, and those who did soon moved on when they realized that he did not understand their tongue.

As Eli fended off the children, Sasha attempted to ensconce herself in the corner away from the press of strangers. She was not one for crowds, and he saw the way she looked at the lichen growing across the skin of their hosts. Everyone bore marks of the strange growth. Eli, as well, was loath to touch it, but could not completely avoid doing so as the children pressed against him. On some villagers, it had claimed an eye or an ear or merged a couple fingers together—and on everyone it left the dark veins beneath the skin on which it grew—but he saw no other signs of sickness or suffering on account of the condition. It grew most heavily on the oldest members of the settlement, while the youngest children bore only faint marks of its presence.

"Just wait," Eli tried to say as someone made another grab for one of his knives. The last thing he needed was to lose his remaining weapons to a pack of children. "Everyone back up."

"You should tell them a story." He looked up at the woman who had spoken—accented, but in the common tongue. "They enjoy stories."

"They wouldn't understand me."

She gave the baby on her hip a poke on the nose, making him laugh. "They would enjoy it anyway."

Eli nodded. "Can you ask them to sit down?"

The woman said something in her tongue to the children, who cheered and immediately stopped rummaging through Eli's pockets. He moved to the wall and sat—the children gathering around as more rushed over to listen. Though the adults mostly continued their conversations, he noticed a few of them listening as well.

"Once," he began, feeling a grin spread over his face. This was one thing Eli would never tire of—a good tale and a rapt audience. "In a faraway land, there lived a pair of brave warriors."

To the sound of drum and woodwind, he recounted one of his favorite tales. It was a story he had told to smooth-faced recruits on their first battlefield, and to children in the towns and villages he had passed through since. Though it was an old tale, Eli took pride in his own unique flourishes.

With appropriate drama, he soon had the attention of his young audience as he described epic battles, dire chases, and fearsome creatures that existed only in legend. The children were enthralled—gasping when he roared and smiling when he reached the victory at the end of many struggles.

As he spoke, one little girl wandered away from the circle to approach Sasha, who remained safely in her corner. Eli watched, not faltering in his telling, but curious to see what would come of the interaction.

The girl reached first for Sasha's head, then her leg, and the unicorn stepped aside both times. But when the girl's face wrinkled with unhappiness, Sasha grudgingly leaned down to whisper something in the girl's ear. She giggled, then immediately threw her arms around Sasha's nose, hugging her tightly. Eli watched the unicorn start and almost withdraw. Instead, however, she closed her eyes and settled into the embrace.

The big soft-heart.

~ ~ ~

It was late when the gathering ended, the novelty of visitors willing to stop and speak clearly holding great appeal. Once the group finally dispersed, Marion was led away to her own quarters, while Eli and Sasha requested to share a bungalow.

"It's a nice enough place, isn't it?" Eli asked as he stripped down for a welcome wash using the small tub of water provided for him.

"I suppose." Sasha nibbled at the sweet grass someone had piled in the corner.

Eli's head was heavy from too much wine, so he poured himself some water from a pitcher. He could feel Sasha watching at he rubbed a cloth over the stinging bites that still covered his arms and back. "How do I look?"

"Like a poxy leper fresh from a bar brawl."

He figured he shouldn't have expected anything else in answer. His skin was burned from the sun, chafed, dirty, and scabbed with welts, his hair tangled and matted with grime. He watched the wash water turn cloudy with just a few strokes of the rag, but the temporary relief provided by the cool water, the momentary ease of discomfort as he scraped off layers of grime—it was beautiful.

Sasha continued eating, throwing occasional glances his way as he dried and dressed in loose clothes fresh from his pack so he could wash his traveling gear. "What is it?"

he finally asked when Sasha's loaded silence carried on too long.

"I think you know."

"Do we have to argue about this right now?" he asked, keeping his voice low.

"There wouldn't be an argument if you just agreed with me."

So much for rest. Eli stretched and something popped loudly in his back. "Which part am I supposed to agree with? We've established that Marion isn't telling us the whole story. We agree that her father may not even be alive. We agree we're about to walk into unknown dangers for a job we have no personal investment in."

"We never have personal investment in our contracts," Sasha said. "Or at least I don't. We both know you get a little too emotional sometimes." Sasha's look deepened. "No, I'm wondering what's happening to you."

"Me?"

"You're changing, Eli. Walking away from fights, not pressing Marion for information we have a right to know."

"I'm—"

"Tired of fighting, yes, but there's something more you're not telling me."

There was more. Eli hadn't voiced it to Sasha. He could barely explain it to himself. What was the point in bothering her with his half-worries until he knew what he was really trying to say? But if he didn't answer her question, he'd never hear the end of it. "I suppose," he told her, "I've been wondering if this is really what I'm meant to be doing."

"What do you mean?"

"I don't know." He ran a hand through his hair. "We wander from place to place taking money from people we don't know to do jobs we don't care about it. Then we turn our backs and move on to the next town. No roots. No lasting effect on anyone we meet."

"You know that's not true. There are families better off because of what you've done. That's why I joined you—it's never only been about the money. You're a... you're a good man, Eli. You help people."

"I'm not certain what I am." Eli tapped on the windowsill. "I've spent so much time charting my own course, I've lost touch with almost everyone I ever knew. How do I know I'm making the right choices if I never stay in one place long enough to watch those choices play out?"

"I think—" Sasha trailed off. Her efforts at empathy looked painful.

"You're still not good at being sensitive, are you?" he said.

"I'm a trained warrior," Sasha huffed. "Talking about feelings isn't normally a requirement."

"Don't deny that you have feelings." Eli looked for a way to ease some of the weight in their conversation. "I saw you with that little girl tonight. Big, fierce Sasha, getting a hug."

"I don't know what you're talking about."

He crossed the room and pulled Sasha's face close, pressing his forehead to hers, just beside her horn. "I'll figure out what I'm doing," he promised. "And I won't let it endanger either of us while we're out here."

"You better not. Whatever trouble you get pulled into tends to affect me as well."

He closed his eyes and felt Sasha's warmth as she leaned into him. "I'm glad I have you with me," he murmured against her.

"Yeah, yeah, me too, but that's enough sincerity for one night."

They separated. "You're right. It's hard to be so close with you smelling the way you do. You really ought to wash or something."

"You poxy arse." Sasha sprayed a mouthful of water at him.

Eli laughed and danced aside. "Careful. I just washed."

"Whatever. Go make yourself useful."

As the unicorn returned to her sweet grass, Eli stepped outside to request clean water so he could wash Sasha down as well.

Chapter 12.
Dark Shadow in a Dark Night

DIGGEN HAD been hunting in and around The Green since he was old enough to draw a bow. And on occasion, he crossed over into ventures that were a little more... creative than hunting. His partners came and went—some to other opportunities, others to a quick cremation and a murmured prayer—if there was anything left to burn. At present, he kept company with three associates—none of whom he much liked. Gimpy was a crotchety old geezer who refused to reveal his real name, drank too much, sang out of tune, and knew the hidden secrets of The Green better than anyone Diggen had ever met.

The second was a girl named Lux who couldn't have been more than seventeen. She had caught up with him a couple weeks back when the crew stopped to trade hides for supplies and asked—demanded, really—to join the next outing. Diggen wasn't going to argue with willing help—especially when it carried that many knives and clearly knew how to use them.

The girl had shaved her head, and much of her body was covered with tattoos he couldn't begin to understand. She also bore a wide assortment of piercings and had a tendency toward silence that easily became unnerving. But Lux was nearly a specter in the jungle and savage as a hellcat in a fight. So long as she didn't murder them in their sleep, Diggen wouldn't lament her help.

The third member of their sorry band was a scheming card player he had accidentally hired a few months back. Turik got undue pleasure from knifing people for their coin purses, drank at every opportunity, and very nearly considered himself the true leader of their group. It was no contest which of the three Diggen liked least.

Tonight, the four of them camped on a dry patch of ground two days east of The Warren—one of the largest settlements to be found in The Green. Diggen hoped they would be able to make a tidy bit of coin there off the pistols they had so skillfully managed to grab from that outsider. While Diggen hated to give the man any credit, Turik's mark was likely going to be the best payday they had managed in a while.

The insufferable bastard sat at the edge of camp, polishing the pistols with a rag while he whistled to himself. Nearby, Gimpy and Lux played cards. They had learned early on not to allow Turik to join these games.

While the others were occupied, Diggen again counted the haul of hides, claws, eyes, and related desirable parts they had collected as the legitimate part of this outing. Already, he was tallying the silver they would be making, and he frowned as he ran the numbers. It wasn't enough—or rather, it wasn't as much as he had hoped. But they had the guns. Never mind that the things didn't seem to work. It was hardly a surprise in this climate. As long as no one asked too many questions about their previous owner, that would be enough.

"You counting those again, Digg?" drawled Turik. "You know they ain't alive no more, right? They ain't going nowhere."

Diggen didn't care to respond.

"Queen's ransom." Lux lay down her cards and claimed the small pile of copper pieces she had won.

"Poxy fingers!" Gimpy hawked a gob of spit toward the edge of camp and bent forward to check whether Lux was cheating him out of his money. Diggen would have given fifty-fifty odds that she was.

A breaking branch in the darkness had them all reaching for their weapons.

Someone coughed just out of sight, a sound that was more announcement than necessity—like the trumpets used by those fancy lords and ladies in the stories.

Diggen realized the other three were watching him, so he cleared his throat and asked, "Who's there?"

In answer, a figure stepped into the light. The new arrival was clearly a predator. Diggen was alive because he could recognize predators—whether animals or men. Most of the stranger's body was hidden beneath a dark cloak that looked far too hot, even for night. He wore boots of dark leather and a broad, black hat woven through with gold thread and embellished with a black plume. The man's face was weathered, though not yet old, and covered with a dark beard on its way to being gray.

Shadowed eyes roved over each of them in turn. Turik at least had the good sense to hide their newly acquired weapons. When that predator's gaze settled on Diggen, he felt himself shiver, every muscle in his body bracing for an attack. No one moved for a full minute, though Diggen's company did not lower the weapons they had frozen in the act of raising. When the stranger spoke, the razor sharpness in his rich voice broke whatever trance had fallen over the others.

"Might I trouble you for a space at your fire?"

Diggen coughed and found that his throat had gone dry. "Might I ask, sir,"—or was it supposed to be *milord*? Those titles always were a bit much in Diggen's opinion, but them lords and whoever tended to be mighty particular about them—"who you are and why you are wandering The Green alone in the middle of the night?"

"My name is Nix," said the stranger. "I am traveling south on business."

No title then. At least Diggen hadn't gotten that part wrong. But he felt himself tense as Turik's harsh drawl cut through the night.

"What sort of business?"

"Private," was the only answer Nix gave. Hearing no objection, he claimed a bare patch of ground near the fire. The man's every move was precise, powerful, threatening. Slowly, cautiously, one eye each fixed on Nix, Gimpy and Lux packed away their cards and settled into an uneasy silence—alternating glances between the fire and the silent stranger sitting an arm's-length away. Turik claimed a seat near them, the pistols tucked safely in his coat. No one dared to speak.

Diggen reached a shaking hand inside his shirt for a flask, taking a long, burning swig of its contents. He focused for a moment on the howling, screeching sounds of The Green to reassure himself that the world had not collapsed to only this dark campsite and this stranger more dangerous than any creature of the wild. Inside, Diggen's instincts were screaming at him to run, run before it was too late.

"There's so much life in this place," said the stranger, breaking the silence of anticipation. "Everywhere I turn there are more types of life than I can count. Plants, animals, people—living and dying—fighting to survive. It's remarkable, is it not?"

Transfixed—like a fear-stunned animal—Diggen felt himself nod.

"A pair of travelers passed this way recently," Nix continued. "A man and a unicorn. Did you encounter them?"

Diggen felt four sets of eyes watching him. This was bad. He didn't know what was going on, but there was no doubt that it spelled trouble for all of them. The foremost question was how to navigate this conversation so that they were all still alive at the end of it.

Gimpy coughed and answered. "I ain't never seen a unicorn."

At least he was a competent liar. Or maybe his sight was so bad he truly hadn't seen the beast earlier. It hardly mattered now.

Nix's eyes turned to the older man. "Pity."

"What are they to you, anyway?" Turik asked.

Diggen braced himself for the violence. When it came, he knew they would be powerless to stop it. All he could hope to do was forestall the moment a little longer, hope that Turik took the hint and kept his mouth shut.

"If they did come through this area," Diggen said, his voice higher than it should be, "they may have passed through Harman's Folly. It's just east of here. Some folk there might know more." With luck, the stories of the unicorn's passing through that settlement would leave Diggen and his company as barely a memory for this stranger.

"Indeed? Then I suppose Harman's Folly shall be my next stop."

In a flash of movement, Nix drew a flintlock pistol and aimed it at Lux's face. Beneath his cloak, the stranger wore a dark tunic and vest, strapped with rows of knives. "My good lady," he said, "would you be so kind as to release the knife you have been freeing from its sheath?"

Lux hesitated before setting aside the blade hiding in her hand.

Beside Lux, Turik had a hand inside his jacket. Diggen stared at him, willing him, begging him, not to be so stupid as to threaten this man with pistols that did not work.

Thankfully, the drink had not done away with all Turik's senses just yet. He withdrew his hand slowly.

"Thank you." Nix stood, holstering his pistol and drawing the cloak around him again. "Sirs, lady, thank you for accommodating me. I will shortly be on my way, but perhaps you should concern yourselves with those creatures just there." He pointed at the pair of black lizards, nearly as large as Lux, which had crept up behind Turik.

By all the powers—

Diggen opened his mouth to shout a warning, but Turik was already turning. He hardly moved before the creatures struck. Their jaws clamped down on either of Turik's arms, drawing blood and screams. Diggen's mind raced to react, but his body was frozen in shock. Then, with a jolt of movement, the creatures dragged Turik into the darkness beyond the camp. Lux jumped to her feet, weapons in hand, but even she didn't dare charge into the night after them. The screams gave way to frantic splashing before settling once more into silence.

The stranger did not move as all of this took place. He simply watched, his face revealing nothing. When all was quiet, he adjusted his cloak and gave them a final glance. "I bid you good night." With that, the man strode from the camp, vanishing almost at once into the darkness beyond the firelight.

Silence remained after his departure for quite some time as the now-trio of hunters stared into the darkness that had swallowed up two men tonight.

"Turik had the pistols," Lux said, breaking the silence.

"He did." As the shock of the attack wore off—it was hardly the first time Diggen had seen such a thing—he found he was going to miss the pistols a great deal more than he would miss Turik.

When Lux said, "that's too bad," her tone made clear Diggen was not the only one to feel this way. No, the tension that lingered over their camp was not due to Turik's sudden departure from their company.

Gimpy let out a cough and hawked a wad of phlegm into the fire. "Anyone else, I'd curse him for a fool, wandering into The Green in the black of night. But that man—if he was a man at all—I pity the creature that tries to make a meal of him."

This was the real issue that left them all speechless. They could only hope that their half-lies did not bring the stranger back their way. Diggen wondered vaguely what the unicorn and the man with the pistols had done to attract the notice of such a threatening hunter. But mostly, he was glad that the stranger sought someone else—rather than him.

Chapter 13.
Dead Adventurers Walking

BREAKFAST THE morning after their arrival was a more subdued affair. A boy came to fetch Eli and Sasha earlier than expected after such a night of revelry. Town festivals back north usually waited at least until the sun was fully risen before people really began to stir. Clearly that was not the case here.

Eli dragged himself off his cot, splashed cool water on his face, and prodded Sasha awake. She nearly bit him in response. But she was never exactly cheery in the morning regardless of circumstance.

When they arrived in the main bungalow, Marion was already seated with Zeti and Zoti before a meal of fruits and pitchers of juice, steaming bitter tea and some sort of eggs cooked with peppers and strips of pale meat. They exchanged greetings while the dim green of the swamp outside the window slowly lightened toward the murky brightness of day.

Eli's energy returned with the fresh food. While they ate, Zeti and Zoti told stories of the swampland—of previous visitors and of members of the village who had gone off to explore the deeper reaches of The Green in years past—folk heroes who had uncovered mysteries both wondrous and terrible. Eli tucked the tales away in his mind. They would be worth repeating later.

As the food dwindled, talk moved from stories to matters nearer at hand. "Our hosts have agreed to replenish our supplies as best they can," Marion told Eli as a few children cleared away the remains of the meal. "They have no maps of the area but have described the landmarks of the course we seek."

A full stomach and a night spent under a roof had worked wonders on Eli's mood—however short-lived both comforts might be. There was no mistaking the sound of the insects just beyond the village limits. "Excellent. If there is nothing more, perhaps we should be off." The options were either to finish the job promptly or call it a loss and wait out their unwelcome exile here. If they delayed too long, Eli worried it might actually become a difficult choice.

"Thank you for your hospitality," he told the elders as the meal officially concluded.

"It was our pleasure. We look forward to speaking further when you three return this way." Here Zoti looked at Sasha who inclined her head in respect.

Before their group dispersed, Zeti made a gesture with his hands, speaking something that sounded like a blessing over the three of them. If there was any truth to the elders' fear of what waited further south, a blessing of any kind would not go unappreciated.

Their refreshed supplies waited for them outside the bungalow—a pack each for Marion and Eli and laden saddlebags for Sasha. As they prepared to set out, Eli scanned the many faces watching them from the windows and doorways of the surrounding houses. One little girl made a sign against evil.

"They looked happier last night," Sasha murmured as Eli secured the bags on her back.

"They know where we're headed." Marion looked at the villagers as well. "And they fear for us."

Well, so much for Eli's pleasant mood. He cinched the straps and gave Sasha a pat. "Don't worry. It'll be fun."

"I miss the raft already," she said.

The route to *tempar gap* had no clear access by waterway, which meant they would be leaving the raft in the care of the village until their return—though the downcast faces of the villagers brought some question to the certainty of that plan. The directions provided by Zeti and Zoti promised that the region would be accessible, even for Sasha, though it would require a great deal of care on all their parts. It was here that Marion's knowledge of The Green would benefit them more than ever.

Eli just hoped that his and Sasha's lack of knowledge about this environment would not work too much against them. He remained, as ever, rather fond of breathing.

Zeti and Zoti waited side-by-side just outside the meeting hall, silent throughout the preparations. As the trio finally set out, the two elders raised their hands in solemn farewell.

"Well," Sasha said as they walked from the village, "There go any good feelings I had left about this job."

Eli shifted his pack to a more comfortable position. "We'll be fine."

~ ~ ~

There was something unsettling about the way the ground squished and shifted beneath Eli's feet as they journeyed south. And not just squished—as the morning wore on, he decided that it felt almost like a living thing seeking to avoid the pressure of his footfalls. Each place he walked left a pool of stagnant water where the ground had appeared dry moments before. Despite the waxed leather of his boots, his feet quickly grew damp.

Perhaps this was how someone went about growing lichen on their own body.

They had rubbed with the oil again, but the insects in this part of The Green were undeterred compared to their more pleasant brethren. Either this or there were simply so many that the oil did not matter. There were large biting flies in jeweled colors and miniscule ones that infiltrated every fold and crease of Eli's clothing until he felt like screaming. Mosquitos whined around their heads while small, flightless parasites crawled up Eli's legs. It made the misery of their journey's beginning seem almost pleasant in comparison.

At his side, Sasha tossed her head and flicked her tail in a constant effort to keep the insects away. Even Marion now waved her arms, swatting at the clouds of vermin stalking them. Three skeletons—sucked dry—that's what someone from the village would find in a few weeks' time.

Not an hour had passed before Sasha whinnied in anger. With a bellow of "Enough!" she sent out a burst of power. The invisible wave crashed against Eli, causing him to stumble to the side as it knocked insects from the air. There was a brief, glorious pause during which nothing assailed them. Eli drew a breath and listened to the stunned silence.

Ahead of them, Marion turned around, eyes wide as she looked from Eli to Sasha. It was her first taste of Sasha's true abilities—a realization that always came as something of a surprise.

But their reprieve was short-lived. A moment later, the whining, biting, buzzing, crawling, blood-sucking swarms descended on them again. "If we survive this," Sasha said, glaring at Eli, "I'm finding the driest, most desolate patch of land on the continent, and I'm never leaving it."

Wherever possible, Marion led them along a twining path of ridges and knolls that kept them out of the stagnant pools on all sides. From the trees, ragged, black birds watched them pass. Snakes darted into the undergrowth and hung from branches. Eli dreaded the moment one would drop onto his head. It was one of the worst things he could imagine happening out here. He ran a finger over the crossbow on his belt, over the knives and sword he carried, reassuring himself that they were close at hand—rudimentary as they were.

"Missing the Furies right now?"

He hadn't realized Sasha was watching him. A short way ahead, she had stopped to look back. Eli shoved his hands in his pockets. "As much as I'd be happy to be rid of them, there is a comfort in having them close at hand in places like this."

Something disturbed a pool of water only a few paces away. The creature didn't show itself, but large ripples lapped at the ground. Eli and Sasha took a few cautious steps away. Yes, at this particular moment, he would have preferred to have his pistols in hand.

They worked their way into a flat expanse of The Green which stretched out on all sides in a misty tangle of vines, swamp trees, and murky water. Some bird screeched in the distance as Eli breathed in the stagnant, putrid sweetness of their surroundings. The humid air stuck to his skin and ran down his back in warm drops. "It rather grows on you," he said, brushing a large centipede from his leg.

"That's what I'm trying to avoid." Sasha quickened her pace to catch up with Marion, who was hacking her way through a patch of vines obstructing their path.

~ ~ ~

They took a break shortly after noon—eating quickly under the unrelenting attack of things that bit and stung— before setting out once more. Now Eli took a turn cutting away the vines and branches that blocked their way. "Marion," he said, making an effort to choose his words with care. Whatever he might be feeling, he owed it to Sasha to handle things more effectively.

And, he had to admit, their lives were somewhat in the balance as well.

But he did stand by his assessment that Marion would not appreciate being pushed. "I know we've already discussed the... sparseness of information available to us about your father, but I—"

"Listen." When Eli turned, Marion had her hands on her hips and a hard expression on her face. So much for a subtle transition in the conversation. "You are fully apprised of the dangers here, as best as I can convey them," she said. "I am paying you—handsomely—to escort me to *tempar gap* and back to Harman's Folly. Whatever you believe about the chances of finding my father are irrelevant. You are here for your weapons, not your opinions."

It wasn't the answer he wanted, but despite himself, Eli held back the suggestion of a smile curling at the edges of his mouth. There was already a lot to appreciate about Marion, and he had to respect that she possessed the fire to put him in his place. He decided to concede the—brief— conversation to her. "When you put it like that—"

With a splash of mud, something landed on the ground between them. Pale flesh, dried blood—it was a human hand bitten off at the wrist. And clasped in the stiff fingers, was the familiar shape of one of Eli's pistols.

Overhead, a bright red swamp lizard watched them with a forlorn look as Eli nudged its lost prize with his boot, before bending down to peel his weapon from the mottled gray flesh. He held it between two fingers as slime and mud dripped from the barrel.

"How is this possible?" Marion looked from the lizard to the weapon in disbelief.

Before Eli could explain, the second pistol landed at his feet—this time thankfully without a hand attached. Even farther overhead, he saw another lizard, this one blue, despondent over the loss of its treasure. Sasha trotted up beside them. "What are you looking—oh, they're back."

"Indeed." Eli picked up the other weapon. "Marion, would you be so kind as to pour a little water over them. I'll clean them fully tonight, but I'd rather not wear them in this condition."

"First, would one of you explain what those are doing here? You gave them up to bandits days ago."

Eli shook more slime from the soiled pistols and gave her a meaningful look, so Marion retrieved a canteen to wash the worst of the filth from the weapons. As she did, Eli explained. "Years ago, I met a wizard. I expect he was entirely mad. He talked about stepping between worlds and the secrets of existence, but very little of it was coherent."

Sasha chuckled. "You did more than meet him."

"Well." The memory of *that* adventure was one that Eli would not soon forget. "I stopped a hill tribe from burning him alive. They were chanting something about a sacred goat as they lit the pyre, but after it was over, the wizard never did explain how he had come to be there."

"Why save him in the first place?" Marion asked. "Was it a contract?"

"No, it was just—there was this crying old man begging for mercy, and a bunch of hill dwellers chanting as they lit him on fire. I had encountered the hill people enough to know whose side I should take."

"Tell her how you rescued him," Sasha said with a smirk.

Eli tried to shush her. "That doesn't—"

"About the herd of goats and the wagon with the wheels that fell off—"

"Sasha!" They were getting off track. "What matters is that, after I got him to safety, the wizard said he wanted to reward me. He gave me these pistols." Eli held them up. Still dirty, dripping water into the swamp, they admittedly didn't look like much.

"He said they would be bonded to me to protect me wherever I went. I didn't question it at the time—mainly because he vanished moments later—but it turned out to be completely true. The—"

"What do you mean, vanished?" asked Marion.

"I mean that he vanished. He was there, then he wasn't."

"Impossible." Marion frowned as she considered this.

Sasha nodded. "It's not even the strangest thing we've seen."

"Regardless," Eli said, "the only way I can be rid of one of these cursed things is if I find someone deserving I can pass them to."

"What does that mean?" Marion asked.

"He failed to explain that part. After my first few attempts at passing them on, I've given up."

"So…" Marion looked at the hand laying between them. "If someone takes possession of them who shouldn't—say, a bandit?"

"They tend to meet some manner of unfortunate end—not always lethal, but the pistols always find their way back to me before too much time has passed."

"I'm going to assume this time it was lethal." Sasha nudged the hand with a hoof.

Marion was still coming to terms with the strange tale. "It seems to me like you could count that a blessing. You have weapons you cannot lose. In your line of work, that seems like it would be ideal."

"Not when every lowlife with a club and a shortage of sense gets it into his head to take them from me. I'm not certain, but it seems that they awaken some level of stupidity in every malcontent that comes my way. I've had people attack me, prod me into gambling, rob me in the night. I use them less now, and that helps me avoid notice, but there's always someone ready to make a play for them."

"But why?" Marion asked. "They don't look like anything special—not compared to other pistols at least. No offense."

"None taken. I know they don't look particularly unique." Eli debated how much he should say but couldn't resist a little theatricality. Holstering the weapons, he waved his hands in the air. "They're also magic."

Marion appeared skeptical. "And why do you call them the Furies?"

The pistols hadn't been quite dry, and Eli felt water soaking into his inner shirt. At least, he hoped it was only water. "It was part of the wizard's ramblings. He said they were 'all the rage' wherever they had come from. I took to calling them the Furies and the name seemed fitting." He adjusted his coat and looked up at the two lizards. One of them hissed at him. Did anything here not hiss?

"Shall we press on?"

Chapter 14.
Those Who Face the Night

WHEN THEY made camp that night, Marion again displayed her skill of kindling the fire with ease while Eli relegated himself to the task of gathering an additional supply of wood. He was determined to learn her method one of these nights. Once the fire was going, Marion spread a double handful of powder into the flames. It took only moments for the clouds of insects to dissipate as the pungent scent of the mixture filled the air.

"Why can't we use that while we're traveling as well?" Eli asked. At least the powder worked, even if the oil was nearly useless.

"It's only activated by fire."

"And if we were to rub it over ourselves or something?" Scratching at the welts that covered his body, he was reaching for any promise of relief.

"You would sicken from prolonged exposure."

"How badly?"

"Headaches, loose bowels, weakness, fever, loss of vision, impotence." As if to accent her point, Marion washed the remaining powder from her hands. When she was finished, she approached Eli with some sort of salve wrapped in an oilcloth. "Take your shirt off."

"So you keep asking," he smirked. Her answering look was unimpressed.

Eli stripped to the waist. "What does this one do?"

"It will soothe the bites. It's expensive, so I've been saving it, but after today, I think we could all use some."

Sasha made a sound of disgust as Eli turned his back to them.

"What is it?" he asked.

"It defies words," Sasha told him. "Your back, as it is right now, may haunt my nightmares forever."

"Don't be dramatic."

Marion made no comment, but she wasn't applying the salve either. "The insects," she said slowly, "have been at you more than I realized."

Now, Eli began to feel concerned. "What is that supposed to mean?"

"Sit down a moment."

He sat while Marion wet a cloth and rubbed it over his back. Pain flared immediately. "Ow, what is that?"

"I'm washing and cleaning the wounds before I apply the salve."

"Wounds?"

In answer, Marion held out the cloth. Only a few passes down his back, and it was streaked scarlet with blood and grime. "Oh." That explained the agony he had been trying to ignore all day. "It is that bad?"

"Worse," Sasha told him. "Much, much worse."

"It's nothing to be worried about," Marion said. Even assuming Sasha was being dramatic, Eli didn't have much faith in Marion's reassurances. "But you don't want to leave it untreated," she continued. "Now hold still." She finished washing whatever mutilation had been inflicted on his back, his neck, his arms, and then applied the salve. As her fingers caressed his skin, Eli wondered what it would be like to have her do the same in better circumstances, away from that snarky smile on Sasha's face—

No, he stopped himself. Thinking like that wouldn't help anything. This job was complicated enough. He focused on the sensation of whatever Marion was applying to his back. It was cool—which was a relief in itself—and tingled strangely as she worked it into his skin.

As she finished, Marion leaned close to his ear. "I trust you can handle your lower half yourself?" she asked in a low voice.

Eli had to hide the shiver that ran through his body. "I imagine so." He took the pouch of salve, and then Marion was gone from behind him.

As she moved over to tend to Sasha, Eli stripped to his underclothes to clean and tend the bites on his legs. Indeed, they were more alarming than he anticipated— weeping blood and some manner of pus. He tried to conserve the salve after Marion's example, but after seeing the horrifying state of his body, he may have used a little more than necessary.

Meanwhile, he watched Marion wipe down Sasha, brushing burrs from her mane and tail, smoothing her coat, applying balm to the bites—of which Sasha had far fewer. When Eli finished, he joined Marion in tending the unicorn's hulking form.

"Have you seen many battles?" Marion asked Sasha as they worked.

"Yes." The word was level, but Eli knew how many stories—how much violence—lay behind her answer.

Marion reached for the large scar that ran down one of Sasha's front legs but caught herself. The unicorn studied her for a moment, then said "you can touch it."

Eli watched. Sasha was cautious in who she let near her, much less who she allowed to examine her old injuries. Marion ran her fingertips over the tough scar tissue and the hard muscle beneath.

"I can't imagine what your life has been," she said.

Sasha's expression softened. "Perhaps not so different from yours. We were both born into hostile worlds— though I certainly prefer the challenges of mine. We've both learned to survive on our own strength. We both bear the scars of what we've faced."

Marion considered this. As she did, Eli looked at her profile—at the graceful curves creased with the worries of a life he did not understand. Perhaps Sasha's words were truer than even the unicorn had realized.

But the moment passed, and Marion smiled as she handed the salve to Eli. "Alright, I've waited long enough for relief. Grab a new cloth and wet it in that bowl." With that, she unlaced her vest and stripped it off along with her shirt, leaving only a band of cloth wrapped around her breasts. In this state, she sat down cross-legged and waited.

Caught off guard, Eli glanced at Sasha. The unicorn smirked back. "Don't look at me. Hooves, remember?"

"Don't tell me you're scared to touch a woman." Marion glanced over her shoulder, laughing slightly.

It wasn't fear, it was... hesitation. Eli's thoughts of moments before were still fresh, but he wasn't about to admit to them. Instead, he only mumbled something about "propriety" which made the others laugh.

"Propriety means something a little different in these parts," Marion told him. "Being a soldier, I would expect you to understand."

Eli huffed. He was making this worse and making himself ridiculous in the process. "Of course, I know that. I—" even he could hear how little his words were helping. Without further argument, he wet the cloth and knelt behind Marion. She tied her hair on top of her head as he rung bloody rivulets of water onto the ground before applying the salve to her bites.

As Eli worked, Sasha lay on the far side of the fire and sang an old battle song under her breath.

We're headed off to fight, my friends, headed off to fight

And come what may, through death and pain, we'll boldly face the night

While she sang, Eli swore to himself that there was laughter in her eyes as he rubbed his hands over Marion's shoulders. She was thin—lean with muscle gained from a lifetime of survival in The Green. Scars marked her pale skin—the cut of a knife, the piercing of a crossbow bolt, some sort of bite. But where her hands were rough, most of the skin elsewhere was smooth, warm beneath his touch. His hands skimmed over her ribs, and Eli forced his attention back to the immediate task.

He worked quickly and handed the balm to Marion so she could finish. Without another word, he retreated to lay against Sasha's side—facing away from camp. And Marion.

"Did you enjoy yourself?" the unicorn murmured.

"Shut up."

"It's only natural," she teased. "Nothing to be ashamed of."

He did not need relationship advice from a cynical unicorn. "Yeah, what about you? When's the last time you went looking for a male?"

"I," Sasha huffed, "don't have any interest in such things, as you well know."

"Yeah, well, my life is complicated enough. And we have plenty to deal with right now, so let's drop the subject."

"As you will." Sasha didn't say anything more, but Eli could nearly feel the comments running through her. He was glad when Marion announced she was finished, and they were able to set about the business of dinner and sleep.

Chapter 15.
A Well-Planned and Noble Rescue

ELI TOOK the third watch, huddling close to the fire for fear of being carried off by whatever winged hordes lurked just out of sight. He heard them out there—buzzing, scratching, sharpening their various appendages for the sole purpose of causing him harm. Before this, it was usually large things which gave him cause for concern. He was developing fresh appreciation for the dangers of small creatures.

When Gnit dropped out of the trees—little faerie arms flailing—and latched onto Eli's face, he shouted a curse and swung an open hand at the creature on reflex. Gnit darted away, and Eli only barely managed to avoid bloodying his own nose. What followed was a great deal of commotion as Sasha and Marion leapt to their feet ready to fight, while Gnit unleashed what Eli could only assume was a string of chirped and squeaked faerie profanity—complete with wagging fingers and feet stomped on empty air.

When she saw the source of the alarm, Marion set aside her weapons. Sasha made a quick search of the perimeter—verifying that no immediate threats lurked nearby.

"Well, hello, Gnit the noble," Marion said. The faerie darted to her shoulder and chattered away more rapidly than ever. Now that the initial shock had passed, Eli realized that the faerie was upset by something more than the welcome he had offered. Not for the first time, he found himself wishing he could make sense of the sounds of the faerie language.

"Wait, who is in danger?" Having completed her patrol, Sasha joined them near the fire.

Eli looked at her. "How do you understand what it's saying?"

"It's not that difficult a language."

He let that revelation pass until a later time.

Marion translated. "There's someone in danger nearby—a man. Apparently, a group of snappers caught his scent. He's climbed a tree, but he can't get away on his own."

Eli watched the faerie gesture wildly. "Who would be out here on their own?"

"A bounty hunter?" Sasha asked, throwing him a look.

"No." Marion kept listening. "A man from one of the settlements." Her brow creased in confusion. "Apparently he came the same direction we did—maybe to try and catch up with us." She tried to slow Gnit's explanation. "Wait, what does the man look like?'

As Gnit spoke still faster, hopping from one foot to the other, the color drained from Marion's face.

Eli felt his stomach clench. "What is it?"

"It's Merrick."

Gnit kept chirping as Eli tried to determine what this meant. "The overseer's guard?"

"Yes."

"What's he doing out here?"

"Probably trying to stop us," Sasha said. "So much for the hope he wouldn't follow."

Eli sighed. This was a uniquely committed guard—or the secret Marion was keeping from them was far greater than he had believed. Either way, they didn't have long to debate. And this was not only Eli's decision. "Marion, what do you want to do?"

"We have to help him." She was already gathering her gear, sliding weapons into her belt. "Whatever he came here to do, he's a good man. We can't just leave him."

Good. Whatever the inconvenience, Eli wasn't in the habit of abandoning people. It made him glad to hear Marion's lack of hesitation. He ran his hands over the Furies where they hung at his sides. "Then let's go see what the situation is."

Sasha gave a groan and stretched the night from her muscles. "This isn't going to be pleasant."

~ ~ ~

The situation they found when Gnit led them to Merrick's ruined campsite was worse than "not pleasant." It was bad. It was the sort of bad that led to sweat-inducing nightmares and grumpy unicorns—the sort of situation that promised injury and discomfort as the least of Eli's worries.

In other words, it was business as usual—except for the addition of the three horrific creatures which filled Eli with new revulsion over the drink in Harman's Folly, even if the name was only in jest. "Those are snappers?"

The creatures were a sort of swamp-crab—their mottled gray and brown shells eight feet across at the widest point. They stood more than five feet off the ground on armored spider's legs, moving in a flurry of joints and talons that blurred through the pre-dawn gloom. In addition to the legs, each creature had two claws which snapped with pistol cracks on either side of two eye-clusters. And between the eyes and the claws, near the spot where Eli figured the mouth must be located, hung writhing, dripping masses of gray tentacles.

"That's disgusting," Sasha said, watching from behind Eli and Marion.

"Those are snappers." Marion crawled forward over the small knoll. The creatures skittered around a drooping swamp willow, reaching with their claws and occasionally jumping at the figure perched precariously in the topmost branches of the tree. "And that's Merrick."

"He's certainly gotten himself into a situation," Eli said. The snapper shells looked tough, and the creatures sounded angry enough already.

"We have to help him," Marion said, grabbing Eli's arm as he pushed himself backwards.

"Of course we're helping him." Eli escaped her grip. "But he's secure for the moment, so let's set a plan. What can you tell us about those things?"

"Their shells are even tougher than you'd expect— above and below, though there is a gap where the top and bottom meet that's weaker. The legs aren't much better.

Those tentacles will keep a death grip if they get ahold of you, and their claws can sever a limb easily enough."

"Wouldn't want it to be too easy, would we?" Sasha asked.

"Eli," Marion said. "I've dealt with individual snappers before, but this is beyond me. If you have any ideas, it's time to earn your pay."

With an enemy waiting just over the hill, and people looking to him for direction, Eli settled into a familiar role. He felt Sasha's smile as he began to strip down to battle gear. She recognized the change in his stance as orders rolled naturally off his tongue. "Sasha, you go left. Marion, go right. I'll move around behind. When I signal, each person attacks a different one. If they group up, assist accordingly, but the goal is to keep them separate and take them down quickly."

"Easy enough." Marion paused. "I should mention that their bites are also venomous."

"Of course they are." Eli straightened his coat. "Everyone ready?"

The others nodded.

"Then let's get to it."

They separated, each to their assigned position. Eli followed Sasha, staying out of sight of the three creatures which remained focused on Merrick. When Sasha stopped, he gave her a pat and continued on until he was a few trees beyond the one where Merrick had taken refuge.

He hauled himself upward, claiming a branch above the apparent reach of the creatures he was about to make incredibly unhappy. Closer now, he could see the guardsman's weapons—a heavy dirk and a longbow—dropped at the base of the tree. Merrick held only a jagged knife as he attempted to wait out the onslaught.

This was what Eli did, and he was good at it. He took a breath, listening to the sound of the snappers shredding bark as they attempted to reach farther up the tree. As Merrick adjusted his position, Eli saw the branches he clung to bending and straining beneath his grip. The larger man wouldn't be able to hold position much longer.

Well, Sasha and Marion were waiting for his signal. It was about time Eli gave them one. He wondered if perhaps he should have offered Marion a little more warning of what was coming, but it was too late to do so now.

Eli withdrew the Furies—the grips settling perfectly into his hands. He cocked the hammers and felt the familiar thrum of energy run through them. Sparks glittered along the barrels of the weapons as he felt himself descend into a familiar place of cool instinct. Beneath the next tree, one of the snappers circled closer.

He raised both pistols toward the creature and fired.

The thunderclap of the shots cut through the sounds of the swamp as twin blue flashes erupted from the pistols. The bolts of energy struck the creature's carapace, burning scorch marks and causing it to stumble. Its legs readjusted as it spun, suddenly aware of the new threat. Eli fired again, adding two more scorches to its back. All three snappers circled Merrick's tree, skittering toward Eli's perch in a flash of claws and legs and tentacles.

Marion's and Sasha's timing was flawless. They appeared just behind each of the other two, ambushing them while the three creatures were still spread far enough apart to be handled individually. Eli fired again, destroying one of the eye clusters of the creature below him. Then, he simply stepped off his branch and allowed himself to plummet to the ground.

Bracing against the impact, he slammed against the snapper's back and rolled off, landing in a crouch just behind. The creature hissed, trying to determine where he had gone even as it struggled to regain its footing. Eli continued firing. He shot at the joints in the creature's legs, at the sockets where the legs joined the carapace, at the seam that ran around the snapper's shell. Flesh sizzled, and gray blood sprayed as the creature swung its bulk around.

Eli ducked beneath a talon-tipped leg and rolled under the sweep of the claw that immediately followed. He heard the claw snap shut with enough force to tear him in two. When he regained his feet, it was to find the creature now facing him, its remaining eye cluster fixed on his position. It scuttled across the short distance separating them, tentacles writhing as both claws snapped again.

Eli fired at one of its front legs. There was a crack as the leg severed at a joint, and the snapper crashed to the ground, sliding toward him in the muck. But as he raised his pistols, two of the tentacles shot out to wrap around his boot. He tumbled backwards and landed in the mud. A tentacle wound its way up his leg—cold slime seeping through his trousers—as the creature dragged him closer to its maw of venomous fangs.

Twin flashes of blue destroyed the creature's other eye cluster. It screeched, and its grip faltered. Eli kicked at the tentacles and managed to haul his leg free. His boot was not so lucky. Cold mud washed over his foot as regained his stance.

They rose from the ground at the same time—blind monster and muddied soldier. Enraged, the snapper flailed outward with claws and tentacles, driving Eli back to escape its reach. The claws closed on empty space where he had stood only moments before. Talons cut through the air in front of his face. He circled away, but the thing followed, drawing closer.

Eli bumped against a tree and slid around to the far side, taking brief refuge there from the creature's approach. Bark and wood cracked as the armored hulk crashed against the trunk. As Eli ducked, the creature lashed out blindly, sending shards of wood flying with each strike of its claws. These things didn't go down easy.

He glanced around the tree. Sasha had her target on the ground, legs twisted and multiple holes torn through its carapace. Marion swung and deflected with cutlass and hatchet. Segments of leg already lay twitching around her as she strategically worked her way toward a killing blow. Maybe it was just Eli who was taking his time. Well, then, might as well finish what he had started—before Sasha came to "rescue" him.

Wood chips sprayed past his face as he dodged a wild strike from the snapper that was now working its way around the tree to reach him. The Furies crackled with energy as he spun to the side, lining up his shot even before he stopped moving. In rapid succession, he unleashed bolts of energy into the mass of tentacles at the center of the creature's head.

The snapper's sounds turned to screams as charred bits of tentacle and armored shell blew outward. Eli kept firing until the snapper swayed, finally collapsing to the ground as its legs curled inward. One of the front legs twitched, gouging lines in the muddy ground before falling still. Panting, Eli kicked his bare foot to dislodge a piece of smoking meat which had landed there.

Easy enough indeed.

Meanwhile, Sasha had joined Marion in dispatching the third creature. As Eli stepped out from behind the tree, Marion gave hers a final kick to ensure it was truly dead.

"Glad to see you still have it in you, old man." Sasha was covered in gray slime and breathing heavily, but she appeared invigorated.

"I'm not old." Eli holstered his weapons. "And I'm cleaner than you are."

Sasha twisted to look at the viscous material running down her sides. "I bathe in the blood of my enemies."

"Don't remind me."

"Wait, what?" Marion sheathed her weapons.

"You don't want to know." Eli feigned a shudder. Marion looked a little horrified. As she turned away, Eli winked at Sasha who shook her head in amusement.

"Are you alright?" Marion stood at the bottom of Merrick's tree as the guardsman dropped to the ground. Eli counted a few flesh wounds, but no serious injuries. Merrick waved off Marion's attention when she tried to examine a gash on his arm. "I'm fine." He gathered his weapons. "Just angry at getting myself into that mess. But thank you for your help."

"Good. If you're not seriously injured, then—what are you doing here, Merrick?" Marion's concern burned away as she crossed her arms and planted herself directly in front of him.

His face grew tight as he drew himself up opposite her. "I have my orders."

"I don't give a damn about your orders!"

"Your mother—"

"Has no say in what I do!" Marion's voice leapt to silence Merrick's words, but it was too late. She stared at Merrick, breathing heavily, but her posture slumped as the statement settled over the group.

Eli really was an idiot. He didn't need Sasha to point it out this time. "Your mother?" he asked, already sensing where this was going.

Merrick looked confused. "They don't know?"

Eli bit back a groan and turned away. The red hair, the power dynamics—Sasha's flat stare repeated her accusation of complacency, and this time, he didn't argue.

He turned back toward Marion. "Dalia is your mother."

"Please." She looked from Eli to Sasha. "Yes, Dalia is my mother, but everything I've told you is true."

"The charges against your father stand," Merrick said. "I'm sorry. I know you don't want to hear—"

"You never met him!" Marion spun back to the guard. "I did. There is no way—I just—"

Merrick didn't respond. There was no anger in his expression as he watched Marion rub her face before turning to the group watching her. "I need answers," she said. "And I can't get them at home because Dalia is the overseer first and my mother second. I know my father isn't the man she claims. I just need to prove it. Please." She looked at Eli. "Please help me."

Eli fought to keep his expression neutral. His heart ached with Marion's pain. He wanted to help her. He knew what it meant to long for family. But there were things to discuss first. "We're going to need answers," he told her. "All of them."

"And bonus coin for the trouble we've been through," Sasha added.

Eli elbowed her. "Let's get our gear and move somewhere more pleasant." He eyed the three leaking snapper corpses and the yellow eyes that watched from nearby pools of water. "Then you can tell us everything you've been holding back, and we can plan our next steps."

Marion nodded. "Of course."

"Good." He still wasn't sure about all of this, but at least they were finally going to get some willing answers. "Now, does anyone see my boot?"

Chapter 16.
Stories and Truth

THE QUARTET returned to their previous campsite to bind their wounds and eat a short meal in silence. While they waited for the full explanation as to why they were wandering through this poxy wetland, Eli tried to sort through his own feelings on the newest revelation. It was frustrating enough to be kept in the dark, but with the truth now in the open, he mostly blamed himself. He should have seen the truth on his own.

From what he knew already, he could understand Marion's desire to keep her connection to Dalia a secret. It did further complicate matters. But did a twenty-year-old accusation change what they had been hired to do?

With the meal cleared away, everyone waited on Marion to begin speaking. "I have so many memories of my father from when I was young," she said, gazing into the fire. "He would tell me stories of the world beyond The Green. During storms, I could huddle in his arms in front of a crackling fire and listen to his voice paint entire worlds in my mind. He always listened when I needed to talk. It didn't matter how big or small the matter might be." She seemed almost to be speaking to herself. "I knew that my parents had their differences, but they always seemed happy enough."

"They didn't want you to know the truth," Merrick said. "Your mother in particular—"

"I will not have you contradicting my every word," Marion said, turning her glare on him.

This conversation would take forever with them disputing every piece of it. "When you're finished," he said, keeping his voice amenable, "Merrick can give us his side of the story—each person in turn."

Marion didn't look pleased. "Fine. But remember that none of it's true." Merrick's face showed nothing as he waited for her to continue.

"I remember my father's smile," Marion told them. "I remember every one of his favorite tales—of faeries and great serpents, of heroes and magic… and unicorns." She gave Sasha a brief glance. "Every memory of my father is warmth and happiness. He taught me, and he cared for me. Even then, Dalia was too busy running the Folly to pay much attention. And I know—I know she had a lot of responsibility to face. I know all she's done for the settlement—but she was always more concerned with the greater good than individual people—than her own daughter."

Marion touched the pendant hanging around her neck—a bronze disk on a leather cord. On the disk's surface was an ancient symbol Eli didn't recognize. Gnit lay curled up, asleep on Marion's shoulder. "He gave me this," she continued, "before he… left."

"What do you remember about that day?" Eli asked.

"I remember that he and Dalia began to fight. It happened quickly. My father told me that he wanted Dalia to understand what was important for our family, not just the town. He talked about the future, about how things would be better. Then, one morning, I woke up and he was gone, and Dalia was telling everyone he was a black sorcerer. There was talk of murder and blood magic and secret rituals. Dalia ran the town; my father took care of me—it's hardly surprising that everyone took Dalia's word as truth. My father was banished before I could even say goodbye.

"And from that day 'till now, Dalia has maintained these lies about him. She won't give me answers—won't tell me what they fought about." She looked at Eli, eyes shining with pain. "I have to request permission to see my own mother, and even when she has time to see me, she doesn't look at me—not truly. It's always the same story, the same excuses, and she gets upset that I'm the only one who dares question her—the mighty overseer. She chose the town over our family, so I'll find the truth myself."

Silence followed—a silence filled with crackling flames and the cries of animals in the darkness. Gnit woke and leaned against the side of Marion's head, brushing away a tear from her cheek.

Merrick took a breath, looking only at Marion as he began his part of the story. "Your father loved you in his own way. No one has ever denied this. He hid his true nature well—from you most of all. But he was a mage, and Dalia caught him in the middle of a blood ritual. She saw it with her own eyes, saw him draining the life from innocent people to feed his own powers."

"You weren't there," Marion said. "You're just choosing her story over mine."

"I've seen the artifacts from ritual, as you have."

"Easy forgeries." Marion wouldn't meet his eyes.

"Be careful accusing anyone of being associated with blood magic, even in forgery. Your mother did not make those evil things."

"Stories," Marion said. "All stories. I knew him. I was there, but you'd rather trust a lie and a bit of blood-stained fabric."

"Your mother was only trying to protect the Folly—to protect you." Emotion deepened on Merrick's face. "It hurt her to banish Aeric—more than you know."

"Don't say his name like you knew who he was. Don't talk to me about hurt. Dalia operates on self-preservation, not feelings."

Merrick's eyes never left the tears on Marion's face. "She has sacrificed much in her time."

Eli did not rush to break the heavy silence which followed, but it seemed that what needed saying had been said. "You are determined to see this through?" he asked Marion.

"I am." Beneath the tears, beneath the sorrow, he saw the determination that burned within. He nodded. Whoever this Aeric was—if he was still alive—Eli would find him. That much hadn't changed.

"Dalia tasked me with returning you to the Folly," Merrick said. "I hoped I would find you willing." Marion turned to him again—defiance written across every line of her face. Even Gnit glared at the guardsman. "But," Merrick continued, "you will not rest until you see this finished, will you?"

"I'm bringing my father home, Merrick."

The guardsman was solemn as he said, "then I will help you see this through."

"I don't need your help."

"It's not a question of need. Marion, will you look at me?" Slowly, tears still glimmering in the firelight, Marion raised her eyes to Merrick's face. "I am here on your mother's behalf. It is not a question of your ability. She loves you and my orders are to bring you safely home. I will remain at your side until that task is complete."

"Fine." Marion's defiance did not fade, though something wavered in her expression. "But out here, you answer to me, not her. We are going to find my father. We are going to prove him innocent." She turned to Eli and Sasha. "What about you? Do you have anything to say?"

There was a lot that could be said. None of it felt like it would do much good now. "I wish you would have told us at the start," Eli answered. "We still would have taken the job, and it would have saved a lot of suspicion all around."

Marion looked between them. "And that's it?"

"You're the one with the silver. We'll see the job finished." And they would. Where Eli led, Sasha would follow. Talk of blood mages was troubling, but it was an accusation he had heard flung at enemies often enough, mostly with no real truth. Magic was rare and blood magic even rarer. As long as they weren't walking in blind, Eli was more worried about surviving the swamp than a family feud twenty years old.

"Good." Marion looked at each of the others in turn, emotions warring behind her eyes now that their course was set. "Merrick, you take first watch. We'll get some rest and press on in the morning. We should be getting close."

Chapter 17.
The Hunter Closes In

FOR THE second time in as many weeks, Jaylin looked up from minding the bar to find a stranger stepping through the doorway. However, while the man and the unicorn had been interesting—a bit odd but fun to listen to—this stranger made Jaylin want to go into the back and hide. He was older and dressed all in black under a cloak that even Jaylin knew must be hiding weapons.

In the shadow under the stranger's hat, dark eyes roved over the few people currently patronizing the bar. Most of those present pointedly ignored the man. The rest stared at him, only to look away when his eyes reached theirs.

With soundless footfalls, the stranger walked to the bar and settled himself on a stool. Jaylin had to stop herself from backing away from the coiled threat of the man's presence. "I'd thank you for water and a bowl of stew," he said. Jaylin nodded, setting the order before the man as his eyes followed her every move.

As she retreated, the stranger tasted the food. "Excellent," he told her, though his expression barely changed. "And now, I have a question for you, girl. Do you think you can answer my question?"

Jaylin felt her head nod in response.

"Very good. I seek a man and a unicorn. They would have passed this way not long ago. Did you happen to see them?"

Transfixed under the man's cold stare, Jaylin swallowed. Why did it feel suddenly hard to breathe?

"Based on your expression," the man said, "I'd bet good gold that you know who I'm talking about."

Jaylin felt herself nod, though she wasn't aware of deciding to do so.

"Do you know if they are still in town?"

"They left." Her voice sounded small to her own ears, and like the nod, it seemed to come of its own accord.

"Do you know if they plan to return?"

"That's what people say." Jaylin had heard the rumors passed around the bar from loose lips to hungry ears. "They took a job out in The Green. If they survive, they should come back when it's done."

"Very good." The stranger took another spoonful of soup. "In that case, I shall require a room. It seems I shall remain here a while longer. No point chasing what will be walking right back into my waiting arms."

Chapter 18.
Home Is Where You Lay Down Your Weapons

MARION SPOKE less after the revelations brought about by Merrick's arrival. Outwardly, she showed no signs of ill-humor, but when they walked, she set herself ahead of the others. When they rested, she sat alone, watching the campfire or the twisting trunks of The Green around them, running an absent finger over the disk hanging at her neck, clearly lost in her own private thoughts. And memories.

Eli found that a part of him wanted to ease whatever pain she carried. He wanted to see her smile again. But this much at least, could not be solved with a plan and a weapon—and those had been his primary tools of action for much of his life. So he gave her space, allowing her to decide when she felt like talking.

Gnit joined them periodically—always flitting to Marion and occasionally riding on her shoulders for a stint before darting away once again. Whenever the faerie lingered, it was to whisper in Marion's ear and make ugly faces at Eli as he walked behind.

"Gnit likes you," Marion told Eli late one afternoon after the little nuisance rushed off to chase a bird perched on a nearby branch.

"I wouldn't be so sure about that."

"Faeries have a unique way of interacting with strangers. But if they don't like you, there's no mistaking it."

"Maybe we should bring the faerie with us," Sasha offered, "as your ward." A squawking sound erupted nearby as Gnit caught the bird and attempted to ride it.

"Only if I get to choose your ward," Eli answered. "Some little noble's daughter who wants to pet the pony and tie ribbons in your mane."

Sasha snorted, affronted by the very idea.

~ ~ ~

That night, after starting the fire, Marion moved to the edge of the camp and gazed out into the night. Merrick watched her with growing concern—but he had made no effort to engage her in the two days he had traveled with them. He sat by the fire, cooking long strips of the snake he had trapped for dinner. Sasha stood by, giving him cooking advice while Merrick's annoyance gradually increased at her suggestions. Only Eli could recognize the smirk curling at the unicorn's lips as she corrected his wrist posture. When Sasha got bored of travel, it tended not to go well for people who lacked Eli's good patience.

Leaving them to it, he approached Marion, settling himself onto the ground beside her. The seat of his trousers promptly grew damp, but he resisted vacating the space so immediately after sitting. Besides, he hadn't been well and truly dry since entering The Green.

Still, he shifted to a slightly more comfortable position, then shifted again—feeling moisture working its way through his underclothes. From the corner of his eye, he saw Marion smirking at his discomfort. At least she didn't seem upset by his company.

Pulling his hand away from whatever was wriggling beneath his fingers, Eli realized that sitting was as far as he had planned this interaction. He still hadn't found the words he had spent the day trying to put into order.

He looked sideways—at her face washed in evening shadow, at the posture of her shoulders which carried a weight he did not fully understand. When no words came, he instead joined her in watching the night descend around them.

It was Marion who ended up breaking the silence. "Is it strange to think of this place as my home?"

Eli considered the question—thought of the blood-worms and the insects, the muck and stench, the snappers and other, stranger things that watched them in the night. But he resisted the bluntness of his initial answer. He thought also of the fears he had confessed to Sasha—fears of having no bond, no ties to anyone or anything beyond a partner and a bag of silver.

He looked at Marion—born and raised in this place— at Merrick who was sliding snake meat onto a plate as Sasha grimaced at the smell. "No, I don't think it's strange," he said slowly. "I think you know when you've found your home. You choose it, and it chooses you. It becomes a part of you in some way that doesn't always make sense to those on the outside, in part because you can see the deeper truth of the place, the spirit that people miss if they're just passing through. That seems to be the case anyway."

"What about you, then? Where's your home?"

"I don't have one." The sadness this admission stirred in his gut surprised him. This job, his conversations with

Sasha, something about Marion—her passion and her bond with this strange, hostile place—had awoken feelings in him he had tried for some time to ignore.

"Nowhere?"

Eli considered for a moment. How long had it been since he thought of anywhere as home? "I suppose I did, once. But those days are long since passed."

"What happened?"

"It is an old story, hardly worth telling."

Her light touch rested on his arm. "I'd like to hear it."

In that moment, Marion struck him as incredibly young. They were near enough in age, but she still had the eyes of youth—fire and strength and hope. Soldier's eyes rarely looked that way. That fire had gone out in Eli years ago.

At her touch, the softness in her voice, Eli found himself answering. "My story began simply enough—as the stories of most soldiers do. I wanted to leave the village where I was born, wanted coin in my pocket and food in my belly. I thought a soldier's life would provide those things. And it did, to a point. But it also brought blood and pain and death—all at the whim of lords and nobles I never met over riches and land I never saw.

"But I proved myself well enough—became a captain with twenty good men under my command. Then, one day, some lord whose name I never knew ordered us to such and such a place. We obeyed, only to find ourselves ambushed and outnumbered three to one. I was injured and left for dead; the rest were slaughtered. I woke in mud and blood, surrounded by the bodies of those I had called

146

my brothers. That was the end for me. I crawled away, walked until I found shelter. A woodcutter found me trying to draw water from his well and took pity. When I was strong enough, I walked away from the soldier's life forever."

Eli remembered those weeks in the woodcutter's cabin—the fear that someone would come looking for him, the anger at the meaningless slaughter he had given years of his life to. "But what remained for an ex-soldier with three pieces of silver in his pocket? I had no real family left by that point, no land, few enough possessions. A few villages away, I found a merchant hiring guards for his caravan. He took me on, and that led to another job. And then another. I outfitted myself with weapons, built a reputation, and I've lived off the work ever since."

"That still sounds like a soldier's life to me."

Eli shook his head. How could he explain? "The difference is that I choose where my feet will take me, choose who I work for and what I do. I understand what's at stake and I walk into it willingly, or not at all."

"Why not do something else? Become a farmer, a merchant?"

He thought of Sasha's picture of him bouncing small children on his knee in front of a roaring fire. "I tried. Bought a cottage at the edge of a village. There was a forest where Sasha could pass the time."

A faint smile curled Marion's lips. "What happened?

"Sasha was bored before the ink dried on the purchase, but she doesn't really have anywhere to go either. After a week, I found myself taking walks that lasted all day. Two weeks, and I started buying drinks for every stranger who passed through town, clinging to any news they could offer. We were there less than a month before I sold the cottage and we returned to the road."

"If you had given it more time—?" Marion's question was one Eli had once asked himself.

"I don't think it would have helped. I wasn't comfortable with such simplicity. Neither of us was. As much as I'm tired of the life I live now, it's a life I understand. Perhaps, someday, things will be different."

"And Sasha?"

Eli looked back at the unicorn who had finally provoked Merrick into a direct argument. The guardsman waved his arms and jabbed a finger at the pan which held part of their dinner.

Sasha had been the one constant in Eli's life for years now. "I always looked for jobs that felt worthwhile—hunting murderers and bandits, providing protection. I was on contract to track a band of slavers when I found Sasha. They had been hunting her through the forest for a week. She was injured—bleeding and exhausted—and still holding off five armed men in a glade."

Eli forced a breath through his nose, pushing down the fury the memory still kindled in his chest. "When it was over, I tended to Sasha's wounds. She was a soldier like I had been, and like me, she was ready to leave behind commanders who held no value for her life. I don't know how it happened exactly, but we formed a partnership right there in that forest. And she's dogged my footsteps ever since."

"It seems lucky that you found each other."

Sasha's laugh sounded behind them as Merrick flung curses in her direction. "Yeah," Eli said. "I don't know where I would be without her."

"What—" Marion hesitated before asking her next question. "Why did Sasha say you're hiding from bounty hunters?"

He had wondered if Marion caught that part of their conversation—and when she would bring it up if she had. "The last job we took—it seemed like it would be simple— clear a mountain pass of bandits so a caravan could pass through. Only, things went bad very quickly.

"The supposed bandits were royal guards waiting in ambush, and the caravan was composed of slavers working for the noble who hired us. Guards died. We fought the slavers off and released the captives, but too much had gone wrong. The duke placed a bounty on both of our heads large enough to attract the attention of every half-decent mercenary and bounty hunter in the region. And even though we know the truth, we don't look good in the eyes of either side right now. So, I decided that we should go where people might be disinclined to bother us—and here we are."

"It sounds like a difficult life."

"In its way," Eli admitted. "But I make my own choices, and hopefully leave others' lives a little better in passing."

"I'm certain that you do." Marion touched him on the shoulder. "And I hope you find your own home someday."

"We're going to find the truth about your father," Eli said. "I promise you that."

"Thank you."

Silence settled between them again. They listened to The Green, listened to Sasha and Merrick hurling abuse at each other over the campfire. Then Sasha said something about Merrick's mother and the argument went entirely, worryingly quiet. Eli and Marion turned to see the other two glaring at each other over the flames. Then, his control slipping, Merrick's mouth curved into a smile which gave way to deep rolls of laughter. Sasha laughed as well while Eli tried to unravel what had transpired.

"Come and eat while it's still warm," Merrick told them as he regained his composure. "Before I give this unicorn the beating she deserves."

"You couldn't beat me if I was sleeping," Sasha fired back.

"I'd give up, Merrick," Eli said as he took a plate of food. "It's useless arguing with her."

"Because I'm always right."

"Because you're the most stubborn creature I've ever met," Eli responded.

"And don't you forget it." Sasha swept her eye over all of them, as though daring someone to challenge her, but they simply settled down to eat. Marion smiled as she helped herself to food, and Eli felt that some of the tension which had hung over their small band for days was finally broken.

The smile really did look good on her.

Chapter 19.
Something in the Water, Something on the Land

THE CLOSER they drew to the region known as *tempar gap*, the less hospitable The Green became—and this was indeed an accomplishment because the pox-ridden swamp had been inhospitable enough from day one. With each step they took, firm ground became a pleasant memory. Sasha in particular had to tread carefully to avoid sinking up to her knees in muck. With each passing mile, the tree canopy grew thicker, blocking out the sun until everything was cast in twilight shades of green.

Dark moss twisted over tree trunks, and heavy vines hung low from the branches. More than once, Eli watched a nearby vine turn to stare at him with slitted eyes before slithering away. And there were times—always on the edge of his vision—when he thought he saw someone watching from behind a tree. There were faces in the darkness, dim forms in the mist that swirled around them—but there was never anything to see when he turned to look.

That feeling of being watched never quite faded, and it began to chip away at even Eli's good humor. "Sasha," he said as another afternoon drew on, "when we're finished with this job, let's never travel in a swamp again."

Sasha kept her good eye fixed on their surroundings, but a wry smile curled at her lips. "Why is that Eli? Warm temperatures, beautiful scenery—what's not to like about this place?"

"Yeah, yeah—"

"I think we should move here permanently. I'll open a shop. You can give tours of *tempar gap* to visitors."

"Yeah, I got it." He shoved her in the shoulder. "This is all my fault, and I should stop complaining."

"It's not your fault." Sasha turned briefly to meet his gaze. "But I do take some pleasure in your discomfort nonetheless."

"Your concern is touching."

"I'm very sensitive." Sasha flicked her mane and returned to watching the swamp. "But in all honesty, I don't feel good about this place." She tossed her head, trying to dislodge a large black and yellow fly biting near her ear.

"Let me." Eli brushed at her face to drive the insect away. At the touch, he felt very little of Sasha's power flowing outward, and his fingers came away streaked with blood. He lowered his voice to a whisper. "You've dropped the ward?"

Sasha's answer was equally quiet. "I haven't had the chance to effectively refill my power since we started this journey. When something happens, I want to be ready."

If—not when. And Eli couldn't say she was wrong. They were dirty, tired, and walking deeper into a part of The Green that was unfortunately everything they had been warned about. The parts of Eli's body that didn't itch, burned; the parts that didn't burn, ached; and the parts that didn't ache seemed to be bleeding freely. Ahead, Marion halted to remove a spider larger than Eli's fist from the back of Merrick's shirt. Eli immediately felt the sensation of something crawling along his own back and quickened his pace.

After passing through a tangled mass of branches and vines, Marion came to a sudden stop.

"What is it?" Merrick asked.

"Nothing good." She moved aside as Merrick and Eli filed through, leaving Sasha to look between the trees. A dead snake hung from a branch a short way ahead. Or rather—part of a snake hung there. When it was whole, Eli estimated that it could easily have been twice as long as he was tall. It was thicker than his leg, mottled in gray and green scales. But perhaps most concerning was the fact that the snake had been bitten in half. Jagged flesh hung from the end of what remained as dark blood dripped into a puddle on the ground.

"That bodes well for our future," Sasha muttered.

Eli saw more reason for concern ahead of them. A broad tree lay toppled on its side—the trunk snapped as though from a blow. The ground appeared disturbed, and he realized with sudden alarm that The Green had grown quiet around them.

When had that happened? There were still insects in abundance, but the other sounds—the animals, the birds— could be heard only behind them. They had reached the heart of *tempar gap* to find it empty in a way that Eli had not yet felt in this place that normally teemed with life— an emptiness balanced against the distinct sensation that something, somewhere was watching them.

"Where's Gnit?" Eli asked, breaking the silence that had wrapped itself around them.

"Missing your friend?" Marion asked, but she sounded as unsettled as Eli felt.

"Wishing we still had a lookout," he answered.

"Faeries don't come into this part of The Green," Merrick said. "Gnit didn't want us to come here either."

"Now you tell us."

"Can we get moving?" Sasha interrupted. "I'd prefer to keep some blood for myself, rather than just feeding The Green's most plentiful inhabitants."

Eli's concerns deepened as they pressed on. They saw other shattered trees—knocked aside as only minor obstacles to whatever had passed through the area. Some had been broken, others uprooted. They lay in tangles of roots and branches alongside the muddy track some creature had carved through the wilderness. Great claw marks scored the ground in muddy ruts, and Eli recognized the sweep of a heavy bulk being dragged over uneven ground. Whatever this creature was, it probably thought of snappers as treats.

They stopped where the ground fell away to the edge of a murky lake below. "Look." Sasha drew Eli's attention to a small island near the center of the water's surface. In the gloom, behind the trunks and vines that covered the island, Eli saw light.

"A fire," Marion breathed. "We found him."

Eli had to admit, he hadn't expected anything quite so normal as the warmth of firelight all the way out here. Perhaps someone had managed to survive—to carve a home out of the fiercest wilderness he had ever seen.

"Don't assume anything," Merrick said. "We still have to—"

The thing that appeared in the water silenced his words. The creature was at least twenty feet long. Spiny ridges jutted from its armored back, and Eli glimpsed rows of sharp scales protruding from the tail that cut back and forth through the water. The four travelers drew back on instinct as one yellow eye flashed toward them in passing. They regrouped a short distance from the top of the hill, and for a time, no one spoke.

Then Marion cleared her throat. She turned to Eli and Sasha. "Have either of you faced a dragon before?"

Sasha snorted.

"No," Eli told her. "Dragons are all but extinct. I saw one once, but—"

"But it might have been a big eagle," Sasha said.

She argued with this story every time he told it. "You're just jealous that you weren't there."

"No, I'm not. I've seen eagles before."

"The point is," Eli turned back to Marion, "we have not faced a dragon ourselves."

Merrick gripped the dirk at his side. "Until today, I thought dragons of sea and swamp were only legend. Marion, we cannot go down there."

Eli watched Marion's face harden into a now-familiar expression. "He's right there." She pointed at the distant firelight. "I'm not turning back now. I can't."

"We cannot kill that beast," Merrick told her. "I understand your determination, but this is foolishness."

"It has always been foolishness," Marion bit back. "Dalia has reminded me of that all my life. I'm a fool for dreaming of lands beyond these borders. I'm a fool for

155

believing that my father is a good man. I'm a fool for believing that he loves me. Well, I stopped believing her long ago. Stay or follow, Merrick, but do not presume to tell me what I cannot do." Marion faced the guardsman, her chest heaving as she refused to withdraw from his gaze. Merrick stared back, jaw tight, arms crossed over his chest.

"What if," Eli offered, trying to organize his thoughts, "we didn't have to kill it?"

Sasha groaned. "Please don't tell me you have a plan?"

"Shut up, it's a good plan."

"You always say that."

"Look," Eli pointed at the lake. "There's someone on that island, right? Whoever it is must be able to come and go."

"Unless they only travel when the creature leaves," Merrick said.

"True," Eli admitted. "But we can at least investigate. We circle the lake, look for signs of someone crossing—a dock, a path, footprints on the beach—anything that might give us an idea how to proceed. With more information, we can decide our options."

"We should stow our packs here," Sasha said. "If anything happens, we'll need the mobility." Eli nodded.

Marion's voice was still hard. "Merrick and I will go left."

Eli hesitated, unsure if keeping them together was the best course, but she was already braced to argue, and they didn't have the time. Merrick nodded his acceptance, and it was settled. "Go right," he told them. "Sasha and I are better suited for the left." Marion glanced at the unicorn's blind left eye and nodded.

"Keep quiet," Eli told them, "and don't take risks. When we meet on the other side, we'll assess the matter again."

"Yes, mother," Sasha said with a smirk.

"We're wasting daylight." Marion nodded at Eli and unslung her pack. She checked that all her weapons were in place, then clambered down the hillside without another word. Merrick offered a tight smile and followed her. At his shoulder, Eli heard Sasha murmur a soldier's blessing. "Tread well, strike true. May fates and powers see fit to grant you another sunrise."

Eli patted her neck and dragged his gaze away from where the others had gone. "Let's go."

They picked a path down to the water's edge, careful to keep some distance between themselves and the gray water that whispered of something moving beneath the surface. Distantly, firelight continued to flicker between the trees.

"Do you think it's really her father?" Sasha whispered.

"I don't know." Eli almost thought he could see the shape of a cottage nestled at the center of the island. "And what feels worse is that I'm not sure which answer I hope is true."

The answers to Marion's questions could just as easily pierce her heart as bring her comfort. He had seen that truth play out enough times in the past.

Insects whined around their ears as they crept forward. Eli searched the ground for any clue regarding safe passage to the lump of dirt and rock at the center of the lake but saw only scourge marks from whatever creature dwelt beneath the water. Ripples of movement lapped at the shore.

"Do you feel like we're being watched?" Sasha murmured.

Eli nodded. His skin prickled in warning, every muscle in his body tense against the threat he could not see. Instinct told him danger was approaching and approaching rapidly. That was all he needed to know. He readied the Furies, triggering crackles of blue energy along the barrels.

Sasha's nostrils flared. "Eli."

Every ripple of movement across the lake could signal danger. "Yes, Sasha?"

"I want to tell you something, just in case this all goes bad."

He felt the thrum of Sasha's magic as she readied herself for whatever was approaching. "What is it?"

"Your plans really are the worst."

The lake in front of them erupted in water and foam as a bone-shaking roar sundered the air. The swamp dragon—even larger than Eli had estimated—flung itself onto the land in a flash of teeth and claws. Eli stumbled under a blast of power as Sasha threw the creature sideways. Unicorn and gunslinger darted in the opposite direction as the beast slammed to the ground.

Every inch of the creature was armored with scales and spines likely sharp as any sword. It dragged itself up onto six legs—each of which ended with claws that could tear Eli in two. It had fins on its head and legs, rows of crooked teeth that snapped shut with the sound of a thunderclap, and a bladed tail that gouged trenches in the ground behind it. Yellow eyes turned to face Sasha and Eli.

Then it charged.

On six legs, it nearly flew toward them—closing the distance in a fraction of the time Eli had anticipated. He fired his pistols and watched bolts of energy dissipate against the creature's scales. He aimed for its eyes, its mouth—but nothing slowed the beast's approach.

It leapt forward, throwing itself over the remaining distance. In a blur of movement, Eli realized that the creature's jaws would close around him before he could move. In that brief moment, he was surprised to find that he still had time to consider how much he truly, deeply hated The Green.

Sasha's power slammed downward. Eli's knees threatened to buckle, but he kept his feet as the creature crashed into the mud at the water's edge. It snarled, and its feet tore up the ground in a vain effort to reach them. Water sprayed around them from a sweep of its tail.

"How long can you hold it?"

Sasha let out a bellow that Eli took to mean "get moving, you poxy idiot!" He raised the pistols and unleashed a barrage of energy at the creature's head. It screamed as gunshots split the air and bolt after bolt of energy hit it in the face.

Eli kept firing, kept pulling the triggers as the barrels of his pistols began to glow red with heat. He sensed Sasha straining beside him with the effort of holding the beast in place.

Water washed over them as a second creature erupted from the lake. It threw itself forward, jaws closing around Sasha's neck before unicorn or soldier recognized the threat. In the moment that Eli turned to check Sasha, the first swamp dragon lunged forward. Eli dodged its bite, but a sweep of its head caught him in the side. He flew through the air and crumpled into a heap against a nearby tree as pain burned through his body.

Shoving himself to his feet, Eli saw Sasha still struggling against the creature at her throat. Her magic kept it from biting through her neck, but she wouldn't be able to hold it off for long. The first creature still had its sights set on Eli.

He turned as the beast raced toward him and barely made it into the tree as the creature's talons tore long strips of bark from the trunk under his feet. Momentarily secure, he balanced on a branch and assessed the situation—trying to determine his next move, or if they were well and truly going to die this time.

Marion and Merrick were racing around the edge of the lake and would reach them in a few moments. Closer at hand, Sasha threw off the second swamp dragon. She lunged forward to drive her horn into its skull, but the blow glanced off. The creature took her stumble as an opportunity to swing around, slamming its tail into her side. She screamed in pain, stumbling sideways as the creature turned back to clamp its jaws on her leg.

Anger burned through Eli—blood rage and fury. He settled into a quieter place amidst the rush of instinct and emotion and shoved the pistols into his holsters. Another tree stood within reach, and he leapt into its branches—his fingers clamping down on the damp bark and moss that gave way beneath his grip.

There was a snarl at his feet as the swamp dragon gave chase, and Eli jumped again. He would never outdistance the thing that hunted him like this, but it kept him out of reach, gave him a moment to form a plan of action.

But no ideas came. If his guns were useless, the rest of their weapons likely were as well. Sasha's magic had effect enough, but her reserves had to be nearly depleted. Already, he saw her stumbling back from the second creature as it turned its attention to Marion and Merrick's arrival.

Eli drew one pistol and fired again, trying to hit the eye, the nostril, the knee—any part of the creature below him that might be weak. Nothing worked. It roared again, sweeping its tail against the trunk of the tree that sheltered him. Eli heard a crack of splintering wood and felt the tree lurch. Wood creaked and groaned before shattering completely. The tree fell, and he threw himself forward, over the creature. He landed in a roll and was already moving back toward Sasha as he regained his feet. A snarl followed on his heels as the creature shook the ground with its pursuit.

Reaching the others, Eli unleashed a flurry of shots from his guns to keep the second beast from taking off Merrick's leg. "We need to get out of here!" the guardsman said.

"Find a way to kill them," Marion snarled, hacking at the creature's foot with her hatchet.

Sasha was bleeding and exhausted. She continued wielding her magic in invisible bursts that knocked the swamp dragons aside and turned their jaws away from inflicting mortal wounds. But she was tiring, and the second creature was about to reach them. The battle would be over in moments, and not in their favor.

Eli dodged a swipe of the first dragon's tail and found himself pressed against Sasha's side. She forced her energy against the farther dragon, kicking at the nearer one with her rear hooves. Both creatures stumbled away, and one turned toward Marion. Eli felt Sasha's power flicker and dim.

So, this was how it ended? It wasn't what he imagined—but then, it so rarely was.

In a moment's pause, Sasha turned her good eye to look at Eli. "It has been an honor," she said.

"The honor was mine," he answered. It truly was.

He jumped over a snap of the first creature's jaws, landing with both feet between its eyes. It tossed its head and Eli crashed backwards against the ground. Sasha narrowly deflected the creature's following attack as Eli saw Marion go down before the other dragon. Merrick leapt to her side, wrapping his arms around the creature's jaws to hold them shut. It bucked and hissed, trying to throw him off.

With a yell, Merrick lost his grip and fell on his back in the edge of the lake. The creature nearer him snarled and spun, reaching him in moments. Its jaws opened to bite him in half, and Eli heard Marion scream the guardsman's name.

Flame erupted all around them. It scorched Eli's skin as he ducked against Sasha's side. The last remnants of her power helped keep the heat at bay as Eli tried to determine where the fire had come from. It roared everywhere—swirling overhead, sending up columns of steam from the edge of the lake—but how?

Then Eli saw the answer.

It was Marion. With blood running from a gash in her side and her face spattered with mud, she raised her empty hands against the swamp dragons. Flame rolled from her fingertips, flaring against the armor of the two creatures. They hissed and snapped, flailing as both turned their attention to her.

Marion screamed, and Eli had to look away as the flames flared even brighter. The heat continued to climb, to the point where he thought his clothes might combust. He buried his face in Sasha's side and held tightly to her as Marion's screams and the roar of flame drowned out everything around them.

Then there was silence.

When Eli looked up, he saw the tail of the second swamp dragon vanishing into the trees. A scorched trail led from the water's edge to the point where the creatures had disappeared, and trees smoldered from the blast of flame that had chased the beasts away.

Closer at hand, Merrick knelt on the ground beside Marion. She was barely conscious—murmuring half-words as Merrick cradled her head. Eli saw holes smoldering in her clothes, and the lower halves of her sleeves had completely burned away. Her face was red, drenched in sweat. Blood continued to drip from her side.

"Get water," Merrick said. Eli ran back to their bags. Now that the fight was finished, he found himself on unsteady legs and bleeding from wounds he hadn't realized he'd received.

Their packs were undisturbed, and he grabbed two waterskins, returning to the lakeside as quickly as he could. Merrick tipped a trickle of water into Marion's mouth, and her movements stilled as she relaxed into his arms, her breaths coming more easily.

"What did she do?" Eli asked.

Merrick looked at him. "I wish I knew."

Eli's body hurt. Merrick bled from a cut above his eye. Blood covered the guardsman's arms, and a tear in the leg of his trousers likely concealed another wound. Sasha, as well, dripped blood as she stood panting beside Eli. However, she met Eli's eyes when he turned to her. "You alright?"

"I'll live," she said.

"Thank you." Eli lay a hand on her neck. Sasha closed her eyes and nodded her acknowledgement.

A strange voice interrupted them. "Well, now," said the man. "That was indeed a sight to rival anything I have yet seen." One hand jumped to a pistol as Eli turned to face the stranger who stood on a raft at the water's edge. How he had arrived there so quietly, Eli did not know.

The man was over fifty years of age. From the waist down, he wore a wrap of some rough material. Above the waist, he was naked, save for necklaces of skulls and bones, flowers and rocks and carved symbols. A gray beard covered the man's face, and his dark hair was tied back with a piece of cord. Though weathered, his face was a handsome one, but Eli saw black lichen growing out from the corner of the man's mouth and twining intricate patterns across his chest. And his eyes—the man's eyes were clear and intense, studying Eli and the others with unblinking focus.

"Aeric?" The guardsman seemed unsure whether he should grab a weapon or welcome the arrival of the man they sought.

Marion's father turned those eyes on Merrick before looking to the woman in the guardsman's arms. Whatever was going on behind that gaze, Eli could not read it.

"Come," Aeric said. "We'll go to my home. I imagine we have much to discuss."

Chapter 20.
Truth and Lies

AERIC'S CABIN offered sparse but surprising comfort considering the location. Eli had anticipated more... growth from a swampland attempting to retake its territory. Instead, their unexpected host led them into a cozy single room nestled securely among a few willow trees at the center of the small island. A bed stood in the corner and a cookfire crackled in the hearth. Shuttered windows and a thatched roof kept out the elements—and the bugs. It was a little stuffy, but as dry as anywhere Eli had been in The Green. Their battered company lowered themselves onto coarse pillows and shared a relieved breath as Aeric set out food and water and rags with which to tend their wounds.

Marion was still recovering from her exertion on the beach—which Eli had not yet come to terms with—and no one seemed entirely certain what to say. Aeric busied himself about the shack, supporting himself always on a heavy, wooden cane. Marion sipped at a mug of water, her eyes never leaving the father she had come so far to find.

Aeric muttered to himself as he worked and seemed to be avoiding looking at them. But after all this time—if he had truly been alone this long—Eli could hardly fault him for his uncertainty. No one wanted to be the first to speak, and so the multitude of questions burned, unasked in the air around them.

Finally, their host set out the last of their meal and took a seat across from Marion, between Merrick and Sasha. He sat uncomfortably, and still said nothing.

Eli shouldn't have been surprised that it was Sasha who finally decided to break the silence. "You truly are a mage, aren't you?"

Considering that magic was most often passed through bloodlines, Eli had arrived at the same conclusion. He was still deciding what it meant.

Aeric studied the unicorn with a scholar's appraisement. "I am."

It was one more thing that had been kept from them. He turned to Marion, but some of his anger faded as he took in how ragged she looked, how raw—and still full of hope. "You knew the truth," he told her.

She nodded. "I suspected. After I discovered my own powers."

Now, Aeric did look at her. There was something in his eyes, something that Eli could not identify. It worried him, as did these new developments. He thought back to all the times Marion had kindled fires that wouldn't even spark for him. "Your bloodline," he said. "If Dalia never showed any signs of power, you would have known where it came from."

"It started when I was twelve," Marion admitted. "But not... I've never done anything like I did today."

"Magic has a way of coming to your aid when you need it most," Aeric said. His voice was soft, but Eli thought he sensed power beneath it—something stirring beneath the surface, opening its eye after a long sleep.

"You promised us the truth," Sasha told Marion, with none of Eli's gentleness, "and withheld it. Again." The unicorn was angry, and likely as unsettled as Eli felt. He tried

to judge what she would do next—whether she would follow his lead.

Marion swept her eyes over all of them. "I'm sorry.
I've never told anyone about my powers. The truth would
only feed Dalia's lies."

Aeric frowned. "What lies?"

"She claims you embraced blood magic," Marion said,
"that you were a threat to the settlement."

Anger flickered on Aeric's face. "I wish things had
been different. I wish I had never left. I should have stayed,
should have fought for what mattered."

"It's not true, is it?" Marion asked. "You never did any
of the things she claimed?"

Aeric's gaze was unflinching. "Your mother and I always had different views of the world, but we began as
partners, in our way. We kept my magic a secret because
there are many who distrust mages on principal. But with
time, our fighting grew worse. Your mother used what she
knew to try and control me."

"So you left me—with her?"

"I wanted to return," Aeric said. "But you were just a
girl. I didn't know if you would want any part of me, didn't
know what lies your mother was filling your head with.
There was too much at risk. But you're here now. We have
another chance."

Tears ran down Marion's face as her emotions pushed
against their restraints. "I'm here," she agreed. "After all
this time, I've found you."

Aeric smiled, clasping Marion's hands across the table. Eli searched his expression, looking for emotion to

match Marion's—looking for reassurance that this was the ending they had all been working toward. Perhaps it was just The Green—the exhaustion and the atmosphere weighing on him—but he didn't see what he was looking for.

"Eat," Aeric told them, as he and Marion released each other. He focused this statement on his daughter in particular. "Magic drains your strength. Recover, and in time I can begin training you properly. Now that you have tasted your true potential, the rest will come more easily."

Marion nodded, apparently too overcome with emotion to respond. As she ate, she traced a finger over the disk she wore at her throat.

Aeric noticed the gesture. "You kept it?"

"I never take it off. It was all I had left of you."

Merrick said nothing, only watched the exchange with an expression that echoed Eli's own concerns. And Sasha's tension did not fade. She didn't eat, only scrutinized each fixture of the house in turn. Dead birds and fish hung at the windows. There were skulls nailed to the walls, books and papers piled on every spare surface. Eli could not imagine spending twenty years alone in such a place. It was so close, so cut off from—everything.

"What happens now?" Merrick asked, again breaking the stillness that hung so heavily around them.

Marion directed her answer to her father. "Now we return home. If not to the Folly, then to one of the other settlements. You don't have to be alone anymore."

"I'm sorry," Aeric said, "but I can't."

"Why not?" Marion's voice caught, and Eli saw the plea in her face. "I came all this way to find you."

"I know. And I am glad you did. But I would not be welcome in Harman's Folly or any settlement. The world is too full of people who fear what they do not understand."

"Then what do we do?"

"Stay," he said. "Stay here with me."

Marion looked torn. Her gaze traveled over Aeric's face, over the house in which they sat. She wrapped her arms around herself as she weighed the choice laid out before her. Though it clearly pained him, Merrick kept his silence. Eli did the same.

His instincts warned him that something was wrong about this situation—but it was Marion's reunion, and he wouldn't disturb that for a feeling he couldn't identify. This was her decision to make. She had proven herself capable a dozen times over already.

Sasha met his gaze, her eye widening meaningfully.

With the silence stretching out, Aeric stood abruptly. "Come with me for a moment," he told Marion.

"Maybe—" The word slipped from Eli's lips automatically.

Sasha cut him off. "I think they could use a moment alone, don't you?" She gave him another look.

Focused on her father, Marion seemed hardly to notice the others' behavior. She rose and followed Aeric from the house. The moment the door snapped shut, Sasha crossed the room to a table piled high with papers and clay jars.

Merrick still watched the door. "I don't like this."

"Me neither." Eli joined Sasha. "What is it?"

The papers appeared to be mostly notes of Aeric's own creation—language and runes Eli could not decipher scribbled in homemade inks that flaked and blotted the moldering papers. In the middle of the table lay an ancient, leather tome written in a script that bore no relation to the common tongue. It was this volume which held Sasha's attention.

Merrick joined them at the table. "What does it say?"

"It describes a ritual," Sasha said, her voice low. "A blood magic ritual."

Despite the heat, Eli felt himself go cold at her words. Cautiously, Merrick opened one of the clay jars. With a curse, he pulled back, accidentally knocking it over. Blood streamed across the table, covering the papers and dripping on the floor. Eli saw an eyeball looking out at him from the dark inside of the container. "We need to leave."

Merrick nodded. "Let me get Marion. Can you two distract Aeric while I tell her what's happening?"

"He won't just let us leave," Sasha pointed out.

All three turned as the door clicked shut. "No," said Aeric, "I'm afraid that won't be possible."

Marion looked from her father to Eli and the others—to the blood running onto the floor behind them. "Father," she said, "what's going on?"

The anxiousness Eli had felt burned away in a sudden rush of anger. He fixed his eyes on Aeric—a murderer who had lied to his own flesh and blood, the daughter who had risked so much to find him again. This was how he repaid all her hopes, her unwavering trust? "Do you know why blood magic is so abhorrent?" Eli asked Marion.

"It is evil," Marion said.

"No, daughter," Aeric said. "That is a lie told by those who live in fear and judgment."

"It is abhorrent," Sasha cut in, anger rippling in every word, "because it allows the user to rip power from the life force of others. It can be stronger than other types of magic, but at great cost."

Eli continued. "And the more powerful the life force of the subject, the more power there is to be gained—isn't that right, Aeric?"

"That's right." The mage's face had gone hard—and behind the expression, Eli saw wildness and animal violence. "But for those strong enough to bear the cost, the rewards are indescribable."

Marion took a step away. "It's all true?" Eli watched her shattered hopes cascade down her face.

Merrick flicked his eyes toward her. "He's everything your mother claimed. I'm sorry."

"He doesn't love you, Marion," said Sasha. "He wants your strength for himself. Since you are of his blood, he can reach the source of your power in a way he can't with anyone else."

"That's where you're wrong." Each word from Aeric's mouth was a curse. "I don't want to harm her. I want to train her. I'm the only one who can. The rest of the world would control us, force us to deny what is rightfully ours. Here, we are free of such fears. Here, we can explore the truth of what we are."

Lies. Maybe Aeric believed it for the moment, perhaps not. But his lust for power would never be satisfied. It would consume Marion one way or another. And Eli had no plans to let that happen. His fingers itched to grab his weapons as he settled into a battle stance, watching Aeric's movements. Merrick had one hand on the dirk at his belt. On Eli's other side, Sasha tensed to act at a moment's notice.

Marion did not move. She stood, staring, seemingly transfixed on her father. Aeric swept his eyes over all of them. "You're just like everyone else," he said. "Weak cowards who seek to destroy your betters for your own comfort. You don't understand this power because you've never known it. Thankfully, my daughter can make her own choices."

Marion's face was a battlefield of grief and confusion. She looked around the room at the violence primed to explode. "All those years ago," Marion said, "Dalia told me that you murdered people, that you were using them for…" she shuddered. "Is it true?"

"Weak creatures are made to feed the strong," Aeric said. "Look outside this house. Such is the way of the world. Daughter, you are more powerful than you know. I can show that to you. After all this time, don't throw away your birthright."

Marion stepped away. Aeric saw her move—turned slightly toward her—and when his attention wavered, Merrick acted. The guardsman leapt forward, raising his blade to strike. Eli drew his pistols as Aeric lifted his hands toward the guardsman. The thunderclap of Eli's shot was doubly loud in the confined building. Aeric's power deflected the attack, but it still seared a line across the bare flesh of his arm.

It was not enough to stop the mage. Power surged from Aeric's fingers—black smoke and scarlet death. "No!" Marion cried out and raised her arms in answer.

"Eli!" Sasha pressed close, blocking him with her body, shielding him in her power.

And the world exploded.

Chapter 21.
A Shattered World

ELI CAME to his senses amidst a roaring sound and a blistering heat that seemed to come from everywhere at once. He blinked against a blinding flash and pushed himself to his knees. Acrid smoke swirled around them in a metallic miasma that threatened to make him sick.

The shack was gone. A wall of flame completely encircled the island, enclosing it in a dome of fire and shadow. Where the doorway had been, Marion and Aeric were locked in a hand-to-hand struggle. Aeric chanted words in a strange tongue. Marion—returning blow for blow what he dealt her—screamed her anger, her pain, her betrayal as she tried to throw him to the ground.

Eli's pistol was still clenched in his hand, the second in its holster. Merrick lay nearby, unmoving. When Eli stood, he found Sasha at his back. Her breath came rapidly, every fiber of her body straining with effort. And as Eli looked from her to the dome of air separating them from fire and death, he realized what she was doing.

"Sasha, don't," he said. "It's too much."

She didn't answer, but her eye flicked to him. That look conveyed everything—the determination, the devotion, the affection, everything that had kept her by his side all these years. It was everything that had kept him by her side as well. "You're my home, Sasha," he told her. "Please, you're all I have."

Aeric cursed and the maelstrom of magic around them pressed down harder. Sasha's legs quavered, and one of her knees buckled under the force of the assault. Eli pushed to steady her, holding her until she regained her footing. Her skin under his touch was slick with sweat and blood. Something inside him shook as he felt that blood run over his fingers. It was fear. It was fury.

Aeric kicked Marion, dislodging her grip enough to throw her to the ground. She crumpled and did not rise. The darkness pressed lower, stopping just over their heads as the flame that mingled with it grew dimmer. Aeric wiped a hand over the blood that spilled from his cheeks where Marion's nails had raked his flesh.

He noticed Eli. "Still alive, soldier? I—"

Eli raised his pistol and fired. The blast of energy caught Aeric in the side and the blood mage fell backwards, rebounding off the wall of magic behind him with a scream of pain. At his distraction, Marion forced herself to her feet. She threw herself at Aeric with a primal scream, wrapping her fingers into his hair and dragging him toward the ground. Flame flickered in her fingertips as the air around them surged against Aeric's dark power.

"I loved you!" Marion screamed. "I risked everything for you." Climbing on top of him, she lifted his head and slammed it into the ground as smoke curled from her grip. "You were supposed to protect me!" She was sobbing now, even as she continued her assault. "Why didn't you protect me?"

Power flared from Marion. There was a flash of light and a sound like the splitting of the world. Eli ducked his head against Sasha's side and felt the unicorn crumple to the ground—her power finally exhausted. He landed atop her and heard everything go suddenly, frighteningly silent.

When Eli raised his head, he found Sasha sprawled beneath him—her chest rising and falling in ragged breaths. The magic was gone. In the night's darkness, he could see only dim shapes around them—jagged pieces of the shack, twisted hulks of burned trees reduced to cinders, the distant shore. Marion was on her hands and knees, panting and retching on shaking arms. Aeric lay beside her.

"Is it over?" Eli asked, unsure who he was speaking to.

Marion turned toward him, her eyes glassy and distant. She wiped a hand across her mouth and tried to rise.

"Marion—" Eli tried to offer warning as Aeric stirred behind her. The mage raised himself up on one arm, a jagged shard of wood clutched in one hand. He drew the weapon back, aiming it straight for Marion's neck even as she turned to look. Eli grabbed for his pistols, but his fingers were stiff, slow to respond to his command.

A large rock struck Aeric in the forehead with a thud of wet flesh, and he tumbled backwards, rolling down the incline toward the lake. Eli turned to see Merrick pushing himself into a sitting position. With his furious eyes fixed on Aeric's motionless form, the guardsman spat into the dirt.

"Sasha." Eli turned back to his companion. "Can you hear me?"

"Eli…" Her voice came out in a rasp. "Are you there?"

"I'm here." He stroked a hand down her neck. "You saved us," he told her. "You saved us all."

"Eli," she repeated.

"What?"

"I can't see anything, you poxy idiot. Did we win?"

Eli blinked, then realized that Sasha was laying on her right side, her good eye buried in the dirt. Her pale, scarred eye stared up at him as her breathing became more level with each passing moment. "Yes," he told her. "We won."

"Good." Sasha murmured. "Now, if you don't mind, I think I'm going to lie here for a bit. Warn me if anything approaches, will you?"

Eli could have kissed her—but even now, she'd likely beat him for attempting it. "Of course." He patted her again as warm relief flowed through his chest. "You just rest a moment." On his feet, he offered Merrick a hand, hauling the guardsman upright as well.

Marion was on her knees beside her father's body. She shook with pain and exhaustion and bitter sobs, but her eyes were open as she stared into his face.

"Is he alive?" Merrick asked.

She nodded.

"What… do you want to do?" Merrick hesitated on the question Eli knew they had to ask. The two men looked at each other. There was death in Merrick's eyes. Eli felt the same—Aeric deserved nothing left—but his urge for retribution found itself confronted with a smaller, immovable question. Would more death bring Marion any peace? Eli thought he knew the answer.

"We leave him here." Marion said. There was no question in her words. "Alive and alone."

"Is that wise?" Merrick still held his blade.

Marion nodded. "It was like Sasha said. When we fought, I was able to... feel his power. Like we were connected in some way. I grabbed hold of it, and I broke it. I tore it to shreds. Whatever is left to him, he is not the threat he used to be. All that remains is a small man, too proud and too afraid to be who he should have been."

Eli heard the sorrow in Marion's voice, and he felt it echo in the ache of his own heart.

"Very well." Merrick stepped forward and offered her his hand.

Lingering a moment, Marion pulled the cord from around her neck and tossed the small disk to the ground near Aeric's head. It lay there in the mud, as unmoving as the man who was so much less than the daughter he sired.

Marion turned to Merrick and allowed him to pull her to her feet before curling herself against his chest. "Thank you," she said. "And I'm sorry that—"

"Shhh." Merrick stopped her apology, stroking a hand down her back in comfort. "You did what you needed to."

Marion nodded and allowed more tears to fall. "I'm ready to go home now," she told them.

Chapter 22.
The Friendship of Faeries

LIMPING AND bloodied, they ferried themselves back to shore with Aeric's raft. Nearly all their supplies had been destroyed in the shack, but that was a problem for a later time. Leaning on each other, each step an effort of will, the four travelers carried themselves a safe distance away from Aeric's territory. Once they felt secure, they collapsed to the ground and allowed themselves a period of rest.

"Eli," Sasha said after a while—her first words since the island.

"What is it?"

"I'm hungry."

~ ~ ~

They found Gnit waiting for them at the edge of *tempar gap*. The faerie darted forward, coming to a halt in front of Eli. Gnit's eyes traveled over his dirty skin, over the bruises and blood that covered his face. Satisfied that Eli was mostly in one piece, the faerie reached out one tiny hand to pat the side of his nose.

Perhaps this was what Eli looked like in those moments Sasha accused him of fussing over her. The thought brought a smile to his face.

With a series of chirps and chatters, Gnit summoned a dozen other faeries from wherever they had been hiding. The faeries bore water in bowls formed from leaves, tufts of grass and sweet slices of fruit. They deposited these in the hands of Eli and his companions, disappearing only to return with more.

The four travelers made camp and felt themselves slowly begin to revive.

"Gnit the noble indeed." Eli set aside his drink and offered the faerie a bow. "Thank you," he said. "Truly."

Gnit gave him a grin in return.

~ ~ ~

Zeti and Zoti waited on the steps of their bungalow to welcome the quartet back to the village on the riverbank. Their journey out of the deeper reaches of The Green had been a slow one. Exhausted in body and soul, they exchanged few words until the first signs of the settlement appeared between the trees.

The number of bites and scrapes across Eli's body had reached such a point where he could no longer tell one injury from the other—and more than that, he had truly ceased to care. Every breath, every movement was a fog of agony, and he poured all his energy into placing one foot in front of the other. Even as the village came into view, he felt himself stumble against Sasha's side.

"Giving up already, old man?" Sasha groaned. "I always knew you couldn't handle it."

"You're one to talk." Eli forced each word through gritted teeth. "I've had to carry you half the way here."

"You couldn't carry me if you were a giant."

In this way, they goaded each other into one step, then another, until they reached the foot of the stairs. Even the inscrutable faces of Zeti and Zoti showed surprise and concern at the state of the four travelers.

"Come," said Zeti. "Come and rest."

Eli had never heard more beautiful words in all his life.

Chapter 23.
The Strength to Survive

THEY STAYED a week in the village. For three days, Eli and Sasha did not leave their bungalow—the same they had occupied on their previous visit. They slept—waking to eat and stretch tired muscles under the watchful eyes of the two village elders.

They were bathed, their wounds tended, and voices Eli heard in his dreams chanted words of healing and blessing as they rested. Some deep part of him rebelled against remaining inactive for so long, but he was glad to find that part just as tired as the rest—so it quickly gave up and took a nap. As he slept, he forgot the sorrow they had found at their journey's end, forgot the shard of Marion's pain that had lodged inside of him. Sasha had been right when she accused Eli of getting too invested. He had little to call his own—he had wanted Marion at least to find what she hoped for. She already carried enough pain.

When he finally did emerge into the dim light and un-breaking heat of The Green, Eli's first act was to find Marion. He still wondered if he had any words to offer her, but it didn't feel right for her to be alone.

Besides, he wanted to see her.

He found her sitting against the trunk of a tree—Gnit perched on her shoulder—watching a flock of bright orange birds nesting in branches across the river. The faerie cradled a small purple frog in its arms and was stroking an idle finger down its back. The frog did not seem to mind.

"May I sit with you?" Eli asked.

Marion gestured at the ground beside her. As Eli sat, Gnit fluttered over—frog dangling under one arm—and gave him a pat on the head before darting away, leaving them to their conversation. Eli cleared his throat. "How are you?"

Marion loosed a breath and took her time in answering. "I don't know. How should I be after all that's happened?"

"I don't know," Eli admitted.

Marion gave a humorless laugh. "I wish someone did. What was it all for? I risked your life, Sasha's, Merrick's—all for him to try and kill us."

"Your life as well," Eli said. "That's important."

"What do you mean?"

Eli thought back to the jobs he had completed, all those he had worked for over the years. "I've seen enough people in power willing to order others into danger—often needlessly—while they stay back in safety. And I hope judgment awaits everyone who sends other people to die for their own selfishness. But what we've done here—it was for family. You faced every moment of it with us. That makes all the difference."

"I—" There was something more she wanted to say. Eli let her find the words in her time. "There is something different inside of me. I feel the magic flickering there. I never did before. When we fought… something changed, and I don't know what it means. That scares me."

Eli had little wisdom to offer where magic was concerned. But he did know Marion. "Fear is natural," he said. "But it is not the final word. Not for you." He hesitated, then draped his arm around Marion's shoulders. She leaned into him, resting her head against his chest. "If there's one thing I've learned in our time together," he offered, "it's that you are strong enough to survive this."

Marion didn't answer, but he hadn't expected her to. Were there words enough for what they had faced, what they had survived together? Were there words enough for the disappointment and betrayal Marion would have to carry with her the rest of her life?

Feeling each breath Marion took, welcoming the comfort of her body pressed against his, Eli leaned back against the tree and watched the river flow past below them.

~ ~ ~

Zeti and Zoti provided four young men to pole Marion's raft back up the river to Harman's Folly. Marion accepted with thanks and the promise to repay them someday for their kindness.

"There is no need," Zeti told them.

"Take our kindness," Zoti added, "and pay it to others."

They said their goodbyes and settled in for the journey back to the Folly. It wasn't home, but Eli was ready to see it again nonetheless.

Besides—he glanced at Sasha where she had taken it upon herself to advise Merrick how to sharpen his weapons—at least he wouldn't be alone.

Chapter 24.
A Final Inconvenience

HARMAN'S FOLLY looked very much the same when Eli and the others reached it. At midday, the streets were as busy as they were likely to get in a settlement that was probably a mistake to build in the first place—in the middle of an unforgiving swamp that ate fools without remorse.

Walking up the dirt track toward the nearest buildings, Eli glimpsed a sandy-haired head ducking through a doorway and heard the door latch securely. Merrick led their group up the street as a dozen pairs of curious eyes followed their progress. Behind the guardsman, Marion walked with slow resignation, her eyes fixed on the overseer's tower—where Dalia waited.

Eli intended to go to the meeting if Marion allowed. After everything, facing her mother would not be easy. He wanted her to know that she did not have to do it alone.

Instinct made him stop walking as they neared the center of town. Sasha stopped beside him. His skin prickled under a hostile gaze. Eli slowly drew back his coat, readying himself to draw his weapons—still trying to determine what was wrong.

Marion and Merrick paused near the edge of the street, turning back to see where the others had gone. Beyond them, standing outside Abasi's tavern, was a figure dressed all in black—a figure Eli recognized immediately.

"Weeping wounds," Sasha swore. "How much trouble are we in?"

"Probably a lot." Eli didn't draw, didn't want to provoke a fight just yet. He and Sasha were both exhausted. Sasha's power was still low, and Eli's body lamented every move he forced it to make. This was not the welcome he had hoped for.

"Well," Sasha murmured. "It's as good a day to die as any."

The figure in black took a step forward. "Eli Craven and his war pony!"

Eli drew himself up a little straighter, but his hands never strayed far from his weapons. He didn't much care for Nix's favorite epithet for him. "Nix the bastard," he called back.

"I don't appreciate that title, Eli," Nix replied.

"And I don't care for the one you've given me, but at least what I call you is true."

"A man is what he makes himself," Nix said. "And I'd say I've done a fair job of rising above my birth."

"I agree," Sasha cut in. "You've made the title fit in a whole new way."

"Dear Sasha. Is that any way to greet a friend?"

"What are you doing here, Nix?" Eli asked.

"I should think that was obvious." Nix drew back his cloak, revealing flintlock pistols at his thighs, twin blades at his waist, and a band of knives across his chest. Eli knew from experience that those were only the weapons he allowed them to see.

Marion and Merrick lowered their hands to their weapons. Eli managed to catch Marion's eye and shook his head, willing her to see the request in his face. He didn't want them in this fight. This one was personal—and neither of the others knew what Nix was capable of. Whatever happened, he needed Marion to survive this.

She held his gaze for a moment, weighing the reality of Nix's presence, before pressing a hand to Merrick's arm. Reluctantly, the guardsman allowed her to draw him aside where they waited, weapons still near at hand. Indeed, the street had cleared entirely by the time Nix took another step forward.

With his muscles aching in protest, Eli settled into a fighting stance. Sasha fell into place beside him, her presence as familiar as anything Eli knew. As in all things, they would face Nix together—come what may.

Sasha spoke quietly as the thread of tension between them and Nix grew taut. "Tread well, strike true, and may fates and powers see fit to grant us another sunrise."

Eli smiled at the words. "That's my girl."

Sasha snorted in derision, but from the corner of his eye, he saw her smile too.

"You know we didn't do anything," Eli called. "The duke wants our heads because we got in the way of his slaving business. He sent us to kill royal guards, Nix, hoping we'd clear the way for his caravan of human captives."

"What does that matter to me? I'm being paid to deliver your head, not sit for your trial."

"It's your business, because as much as you're a bastard, I know you're not one to kill an innocent man on false charges."

"And you're innocent, are you?" One of Nix's hands slid to his pistol even as he flashed them an easy grin.

"Today?" Eli answered, "I would say that I am."

Nix laughed. "That's rich, coming from a mercenary and a soldier. Where have you been all this time anyway? I've been stuck in this pit of a town while some girl tried to get me to drink bowls of piss."

Right now, sitting at Jaylin's bar and drinking bowls of snapper piss was one of the most comforting things Eli could imagine. "It's actually not bad once you get used to the flavor."

"Yes, it is," Sasha muttered.

Eli watched Nix settle into his stance. He took a breath, flexed his fingers. The thread between them was at the breaking point. Next would come violence.

Marion stepped into the street. "They were helping me," she called to Nix.

Eli's heart stuttered, but he didn't dare make a move.

The mercenary turned toward her. "And what, Miss, were they helping you do exactly?"

"I hired them to find my father." Marion risked another step into the street, her empty hands outstretched.

Nix considered her words. "Did you find him?"

"We did."

"Well, congratulations. If that's the case, you have no further need of them. I'll even spare you the trouble of having to pay for their services." Nix drew his pistols. Eli withdrew his own weapons as Sasha flared her power beside him.

But Marion wasn't finished. "We found him but then he tried to kill us."

Nix offered her a glance. "What did you say?"

"My father was a blood mage who tried to kill us. Eli and Sasha helped me face him."

"They do tend to bite off more than they can chew. Judging by the fact that you're all still breathing, I will venture to guess that you were the victors. Did you kill him or did they?"

"Neither," Marion answered. "We left him alive."

Nix laughed, a deep, rolling sound from within his chest as he looked from Marion to Eli. "Is that so? If it was me, I would have opened his throat and left him to whatever sort of poxy creatures live in this place."

Marion shook her head. "It wouldn't have achieved anything."

Nix shrugged. "Might have made you feel better."

"We've had enough violence, Nix," Eli called.

"Have we?" In a swirl of shadows and blackness, Nix turned one pistol on Marion.

"Don't!" Eli responded without thinking. Rather than fire, he ran to Marion, feeling Sasha's power at his back, giving him the speed to make it in time. He placed himself between her and the bounty hunter before Nix could shoot.

The two men stood there, pistols aimed at each other's faces. With energy crackling through his weapons, Eli waited for Nix to act. Moving to Eli's side, Sasha snorted and pawed the ground.

"Can I kill him?" she asked.

"Wait." Eli murmured. "No one needs to die today."

Nix met his eyes across the space between them, and the bounty hunter's gaze turned thoughtful. Then he shook his head. "Damn it, Eli, you always were too good for my liking." He slipped his pistols back into their holsters. "But don't think this is the end. One of these days, you're going to break your poxy code of honor and tumble down to the rest of us cutthroats—then you'll see what I can do to you."

The tension faded from Eli's chest as quickly as it had come. "I've seen what you can do," he answered. "I'm not worried."

Nix laughed again before turning and starting down the road out of Harman's Folly.

"Poxy arse!" Sasha called after him as Nix walked into the trees and vines bordering the causeway. Then, with a flicker of shadow, he was gone.

"Is that it?" Marion asked, watching the point where Nix had vanished.

Eli grinned at the confusion on her face. "That's it."

"I don't understand."

"Nix," Eli said, "prides himself on having an unbreakable personal code."

"Damned if we know what it is though," Sasha added.

Even Eli struggled to understand the grizzled mercenary. "It's best not to question him too deeply. You'll only make your head hurt."

Sasha flashed a glare toward the spot Nix no longer stood. "I really hate him."

"I know." Eli patted her neck. It was then that he noticed Dalia standing at the edge of the street, with Merrick at her side. "Marion." He nodded in that direction.

When Marion turned, her face went a little pale. Eli touched her on the arm, and she smiled faintly in thanks. "Mother," she said, walking forward. Eli moved to follow, but Sasha stopped him.

"I think she can handle this one on her own." Eli still felt drawn to join her, but Sasha was probably right. Joining them would be for his comfort—not Marion's.

They watched as Merrick withdrew to let Dalia and Marion speak privately. First there were words, then tears—but no anger. When Dalia drew Marion into her arms, Marion returned the embrace in kind, and Eli felt himself release a breath he hadn't intended to hold.

"What are you thinking?" Sasha asked.

"I wish I knew." A tempest of emotions swirled through Eli's chest—affection and loss, sorrow and triumph. Nix's actions—predictable as they were in their unpredictability—had only made him more unsettled. He still hadn't ordered his thoughts by the time Marion returned to them, face streaked with tears but smiling with genuine happiness as she held out a bag of silver.

"Here," she said. "The rest of your payment, as promised."

"I—"

"Eli," Sasha said, "if you turn down payment, I swear, I'll go join Nix."

Eli grinned and took the money from Marion. "I wasn't going to. Though it would be worth it just to see how long the two of you lasted together." He turned his attention to Marion. "Are you all right?"

Marion nodded. "I have a lot to think about, but, yes, things are going to work out. Thank you." She lay a hand on the side of Sasha's head. "Thank you for everything."

Sasha nuzzled against her touch. "Thank you," she said, "for not letting Eli get us killed."

Eli elbowed the unicorn as Marion laughed. Her eyes met his and held there. Eli felt each breath, felt the emotions crashing against his chest. Now that the job was over, there were things, perhaps, that he could say. But for the moment, neither of them spoke.

Marion took a step toward him, and Eli moved to meet her. Ignoring Sasha's sigh of exasperation—he leaned down to press a kiss to Marion's lips. Her arms slid around his shoulders, and she leaned in as the kiss deepened. She was warm and tasted of salt and sour marsh air. Her body settled against his, and Eli shifted, trying to get a little more comfortable. He shifted again, pressing against her lips.

When they separated, Marion was slightly flushed. She looked up into Eli's face. He was the first to speak. "That was…"

"Strange," she finished.

"Not right."

"Not bad."

"But…"

"…strange."

"Indeed." Eli felt himself chuckle, unsure what to do next as Marion took a half-step backwards. The emotions inside of him had quieted. The kiss had been pleasant enough, but it had not felt *right*. He wasn't certain what to do with that fact, but it had him quickly reorganizing his thoughts about future possibilities.

"You two are idiots." Sasha walked away.

Marion extended her hand first. "I'm glad I met you, Eli."

Eli hesitated, then took her hand in his. "I'm glad as well. Even if we did begin with you breaking into my room and holding a knife to my throat."

She shrugged. "It worked out in the end."

"Indeed."

"Now come along. My mother wants to thank you personally for your help." Sasha had joined Merrick and Dalia, all of whom were working to keep the amusement from their faces as they looked on. Marion moved to join them.

"Marion, wait."

She turned back, and a question settled over her face as Eli unstrapped one of his pistols. He looked at the weapon before holding it out.

"Are you certain?" she asked. "Can you even give me one? I'm rather fond of having both my hands."

He felt the weight of the pistol in his hand. "You know by now what it means to carry one of these. It's yours only if you want it." He met her eyes. "But, yes, I do believe I can, finally, give you one."

Marion came close and wrapped her fingers around the weapon. As she took it from him, a smile spread across her face. "What is it?" Eli asked.

"I'm not certain. Something about this feels right, don't you think?"

"I do. But we'll see if you still feel that way the first time someone tries to take that from you."

Marion strapped the weapon around her waist. "If they do, I'll just give it to them, isn't that how it goes?"

"You're learning."

"Only one though?" she asked. "I thought you were trying to retire?"

Eli raised an eyebrow. "Getting greedy?"

Marion rolled her eyes and waited for him to answer.

"I don't think I'm ready to give up this life just yet," he said. Seeing Dalia embrace Marion, Nix's grudging admission that Eli was still managing to do some good in the world—these things had helped him remember why he lived the life he did.

And Sasha would not appreciate another attempt at the life of a farmer.

When they rejoined the others, Dalia grasped Eli's hand in both of hers. Though her expression still could not be called *friendly*, there was sincerity enough in her voice. "Our first meeting was not what it might have been," she said, "and I suspect that is in part my fault. Thank you for helping my daughter come home safely. Anything you need for the remainder of your stay, all you have to do is ask."

"You are most gracious," Eli told her.

He shook Merrick's hand as well, reading the recognition in the guardsman's eyes, a soldier's shared bond.

"Well," Sasha asked, bumping against Eli's shoulder. "What now?"

"Now," Eli told her. "I could really use a large mug of snapper piss."

Sasha groaned. "Please tell me you're not going to make me drink that swill again?"

Leaving Marion and the others to further discussion, he dragged Sasha toward the tavern. "Stop your groaning, I'm buying."

"That doesn't make it taste any better."

"Sure it does. You're just scared I can outdrink you."

"A pox on you. Fine," Sasha muttered, quickening her pace. "But just one drink."

Chapter 25.
A Brand-New Plan

WHEN MARION entered the tavern an hour later, it was to find Eli slumped in a corner booth, nursing an unnumbered mug of drink from the barrel on the counter. Jaylin watched from the bar with a crooked smile as Sasha leaned against the wall singing soldier's songs and flapping her lips to try and dislodge the taste of the snapper piss from her mouth.

Marion slid into the seat across from Eli. "So, what's the plan?"

"The plan?" He focused his attention on her and sat up straighter.

"Don't let him make a plan," Sasha said. "Those never end well."

Eli wagged a finger at her. "My plans are the best plans."

Marion chuckled, waiting as Eli took another unsteady drink. Whatever it really was, it tasted better with each fresh mug. He wondered briefly if they could sell it in the north under some exotic name before dragging his eyes back to Marion.

"I don't know," he admitted. "I expect we'll stay in the Folly for a little while—rest and resupply. After that, well, there's a whole world still out there—away from the flies—"

"—and snakes—" Sasha added.

"—and snappers—"

"—and swamp dragons—"

"—and all that." Eli drained his mug. "No doubt there are other sell swords out for our blood, but if we can face Nix, we can face any of them. Regardless, I'm ready to move on from The Folly—"

"Hear, hear," agreed Sasha.

"—and I suppose we'll deal with the rest as it comes."

"Well," Marion tapped the table. "I was going to say—and this is only if you're interested—but if you don't mind spending another week or so in town, I might be looking for someone to travel with, maybe someone who knows their way around the world outside The Green and who might have an idea of how to make money out there? Someone willing to take on another partner with a bit of magical ability that is likely to attract unwelcome attention?" She raised her eyes from the table to Eli's face as she asked the question.

"Did you miss the bit about there being a bounty on both our heads?" Sasha asked.

"No, I've rather grasped that much by now."

The unicorn grinned at the biting sarcasm. "In that case, maybe you're fool enough to come with us after all."

Marion laughed, but her face grew more serious as she waited for Eli's response. "What do you say?"

It was a sincere question—and though she tried to hold some of it back, Eli could see that she really wanted this. She would outlast her father's failings. She would forge her trail through the world and make it a better place in passing. That was all he needed to know. "Jaylin!" He slapped the table. "Another round of drinks! We're celebrating."

Jaylin appeared at the table with a pitcher and a fresh mug for Marion and poured drinks for all three. "What are you celebrating?" she asked.

"To the stories yet to be written." Eli raised his mug in a toast.

"To the start of a new adventure," Marion added, tapping her mug to Eli's before they both drank.

Sasha groaned and slumped against the wall. "We're all going to die."

The End

Acknowledgments

THERE ARE so many people to thank over the course of creating a book. First of all, thank you to Daien Sanchez for talking through repeated drafts of this book with me—and for the writing accountability and friendship along the way. Thanks also to Emlyn Meredith Dornemann, Clifford Royal Johns, Mary Randall, Claire Guyton, Darren Deth, and Nancy Brown for offering feedback on various versions of this manuscript. As solitary an act as writing tends to be, it does not happen alone. You all helped make this story better than I would have alone.

Thanks to Claire Guyton for your editorial eye and to Jess Koch for cover formatting and design. Huge thanks to Darby Mumford for bringing this story to life with such delightful illustrations. I knew from the beginning that I wanted art to be a part of this story, and you helped turn that desire into a reality.

I am incredibly thankful for the Stonecoast MFA writing community—with a special shout-out to my writing cohort, Not Actually Vampires. Y'all made a great program even better. Extra special thanks to Theodora Goss, David Anthony Durham, Elizabeth Hand, Mike Kimball, Nancy Holder, James Patrick Kelly, Tom Coash, Sarah Braunstein, Aaron Hamburger and the rest of   the

Stonecoast Staff and faculty. You all helped me become the writer I am today.

Additional thanks to my library community; the Maine arts, literary, and theater communities; and my friends and family for the support and encouragement you have offered over the years.

There are many more names I could list, but I'll wrap this up. To everyone who has supported me, encouraged me, and laughed with me—to all the dreamers and everyone trying to find your way in the world—you matter.

I thank God for allowing me this opportunity. If all goes to plan, this book you hold in your hands will be the first of many. When I began, it was hard to picture where this writing thing would lead. With this book, I feel a new chapter of the journey beginning.

So finally, thank you, reader, for giving my world-weary gunslinger and snarky unicorn a chance. It's been a delight to spend time with them, and I'm looking forward to seeing what troubles they get into on their next adventure. There's plenty more to come.

About the Creators

JOSH GAUTHIER is a fiction writer, playwright, and librarian currently living in Maine. A graduate of the Stonecoast Creative Writing program, he works across genres with a focus on fantasy, horror, and romance. His work has previously been published in places such as *The NoSleep Podcast* and *The Stonecoast Review*. You can find him on various social media platforms and online at joshgauthierwriter.com.

~ ~ ~

DARBY MUMFORD lives with her family on a homestead in Maine. She has been teaching since 1982 and is presently teaching home school students. She is a graduate of Mass. College of Art and has taken classes at Boston Museum School, Dartmouth, and studied with the Famous Artist School. Illustration is her first love, and she has written, illustrated and self-published five children's books.